We, the Dangerous
Janice Mirikitani

New and Selected Poems

CELESTIALARTS

Berkeley. California

Celestial Arts
P.O. Box 7327
Berkeley, CA 94707

ISBN: 0-89087-767-X

Published in Great Britain by Virago Press. Some poems included
in this volume are reprinted from *Shedding Silence*,
Celestial Arts, Berkeley, CA, 1987 and *Awake in the River*,
Isthmus Press, San Francisco, CA, 1978.

Portrait of Janice Mirikitani © Howard Schatz from the book,
GIFTED WOMAN (Pacific Photographic Press, 1993).
GIFTED WOMAN can be ordered by calling (415) 626-4911
($24.95 + tax and shipping).

Printed in the United States of America.

1   2   3   4   5   6 — 99   98   97   96   95

To Dr. Maya Angelou
and Rev. Cecil Williams
who ignite our tongues

CONTENTS

LOOKING FOR AMERICA

BOWL OF RAGE

WOMAN WITH STRAIGHT BACK

LATE WITH LUNCH

TONGUES AFIRE

Looking for America

PARADISE

Before the lava cooled
we could sing.

Before the beaches died
we could chant prayers.

Now my children sell pukka shells,
eat Spam with Coke and Kentucky Fried Chicken.
I string my tongue
like leis across the necks of haolies.*

> In Waikiki
> A Hawaiian banquet:
> pineapple boats,
> hibiscus floating in mango bowls.
> Sunred vacationers eat
> under white umbrellas.
> A wrong order is served
> to the woman in lime green shorts,
> and parrot printed shirt.
> "This is America!" she screams,
> shaking her fist at the Hawaiian maitre'd.
> "Tell your people to speak American.
> You're in America now!"

In taro patches,
thick leaves like tongues
grow wild,
fed by mountain rain.

Some things do not die,
won't be franchised.

---

*Hawaiian slang for Caucasians.

LOOKING FOR AMERICA

I searched for myself
in the pages of Time,
among the brilliant and beautiful, best sold and discovered.
I looked for myself on the screen
wooed by Gable and Brando and McQueen,
on the tube selling Colgate or Camay or Kotex or Crisco,
hunted for me on billboards or climbing the rungs
of executive ladders,
and saw myself

> being shot by John Wayne,
> conquered by Stallone,
> out-karated by Norris, Van Damme, Carradine and Seagal.

I found myself
> in a bar, dancing for a tip,
> cheong sam slit to my hip,
> or in a brothel, compliant and uncomplicated,
> high-heeled in bed, wiping some imperialist's lips
> with hot scented towels.

I see myself pound my head
on the glass of their ceiling, two rungs up
a short corporate ladder.

I meet myself pigeon toed and shuffling, tongue twisted,
chop chop/sing song/giggle/rots of ruck/bucktoothed/
cokebottle eyeglassed/cartoon camera carrying foreigner
who is invisible

on America's pages.

BEAUTY CONTEST

1.

After the war, the camps;
when we moved to Chicago

all I remember was the cold.

When they called me Jap and slant eyed girl,
I laughed and disappeared.

Momma took in ironing for extra money.
Daddy left for his red lipped honey.

I'm glad we split from Chicago.

All I remember was the cold . . .

2.
RECIPE FOR ROUND EYES

Ingredients: scissors, Scotch magic transparent tape,
            eyeliner – water based, black.
            optional: false eyelashes.

Cleanse face thoroughly.
For best results, powder entire face, including eyelids.
        (light shades suited to total effect desired)

With scissors, cut magic tape 1/16" wide, 3/4" to 1/2" long,
depending on length of eyelid.

Stick firmly onto mid upper eyelid area
    (looking down into handmirror facilitates finding
    adequate surface)

If using false eyelashes, affix first on lid, folding any
excess lid over the base of eyelash with glue.

Paint black eyeliner on tape and entire lid.

Do not cry.

3.
I'M HER

I joined the UCLA campus belles.
or rather I was selected, like in a beauty
contest. I learned how to wear sweaters
just-right tight. how to s-curve my spine and walk
by shifting my weight from my hip so I could
gyrate.
There were two of us "orientals"
which was the quota in this club of co-eds,
perky blonds.
I copied their hairstyles, learning how to back comb,
hot perm, and "bounce".
Squeezed oranges a hundred times a day
to pump my chest.
I memorized their cadences, the octave giggle,
and breathless oooooooo.
I was ready.
With my new light powder blue sweater,
I gyrated among the athletes, the shapely blonds.
Finally, a tight end from Iowa State,
towering like a hero, eyes lasering into mine,

a slow smile crossing his face
says: "Hey geisha mama, won't you get us a couple of beers?"

4.
WILD JODY

Let me teach you some Japanese songs . . .
it's real easy, memorize the syllables, that's all.
You really ought to run for Lotus Blossom Queen.
You got the legs and the face.
It's not like you're competing against white girls.

> *"Watashii wa machi de matte eru kodomo*
> *chi ma ta no ko . . ."*
>   *(I am waiting, a child of the city)*

They'll love the Japanese songs for the talent part,
you know? like you're really into preserving the culture.
            Who me?   Jody Yamasaki?   Are you kidding?
I got bowed legs, my eyes are too small and my tits too flat.
and I can't talk good. What a laugh, me.
parading around in a bathing suit.
If some dirty old man looked at me funny, I'd tell him
to suck his dick. I can't kiss ass. My temper's too mean.
You know, I got so mad once, I nearly killed a guy.
He deserved it.
Lied to me, the cocksucker. Made a fool out of me.
You know how much I'm into cars and my dad just keeps
buying me another one every time I mess one up.
Anyway, this guy and me got close.
He didn't have a car and I really went for his lies.
He had me thinking I was his true love,
his only thing, his red caboose, his doll.
He had a job in Gardena, worked late sometimes
and asked to borrow my car, so he could be with me quicker.

I woulda gave him my arms, curled my hair,
straightened my teeth for that motherfucker.
So one night he gets in a little wreck.
Calls me up, tells me everything's ok and he'd take care of it,
get it fixed.
So the next week the other guy's insurance company
calls me and asks if I'm Miss Tsukamoto.
Who's she, I ask.
She's the witness in the car with my guy.
What nerve, huh? using my car to take out this other chick.
Well, I'm mad and I get in my car, drive to his house.
And I sit out there, blowing my horn until he comes out,
all smiling and everything, you know, happy to see me.
I back up with all my rubber burning, my pistons pumping,
my chassis smoking. He looks like he's gonna pisshispants,
and I'm screaming lying sonofabitch.
GONNA TSUKA YOUR MOTO.
He sees that I found him out, and I'm crazy, you know.
He runs to his house, and I'm up on his lawn,
running over his bushes, ramming his front steps,
honking and yelling deep shit.
All his neighbors and folks are waving and yelling
and call the police cause they see I'm going to
run over this motherfucker. At least I got to break his leg.
I back out and do 90 all the way to East L.A.
and the cops are chasing me. Yea, sirens and red lights
and everything. When I finally stopped
I just rolled down my window and stuck out my hand
for the ticket. Didn't say shit to the cops.
Men. Fuck 'em all.
Yea, so I could teach you these songs.

> *"mado ni aka ri ga . . ."*
> *(when the time comes)*

you gotta have right whachacallit? inflection?

"tomu ro ko ro . . ."
                    (someone lights the candle at the window)

My dad taught me these songs before he divorced us.
Funny, huh? He'd never be around much, or talk to me at all,
working his ass off at that electronics company,
come home late drunk sometimes and singing.
Sneak into my room and start crying.
Christ. I didn't know what was happening,
him holding me, singing to me in the dark . . .
blowing his nose on my underpants . . .

                    "etsu mo no, mi chi no . . .
                    aruki masu . . ."
                              (I will always walk the same road)

Japanese songs are real . . . whatstheword? sad. Melancholy.
They're always about somebody leaving. You know?
Waiting for someone who never shows up.
     Yea, you should run.
You're not competing with white girls and just think
if you win, you could wrap all those guys around
your finger . . .
     Come on, sing: *"Watashi wa machi de matte eru kodomo . . ."*

'I CAN'T FORGET THE FACE'

I can't forget the face,
red from the neck he craned to stare at me.
His snarl grows from his upper lip
and curls around his teeth.
At that moment
I know the intent, the desire
to assault me . . .
From behind his steering wheel he screams:
"JAP! Learn how to drive or
GET OUT OF AMERICA."
And his car? A Colt Mitsubishi.

YES, WE ARE *NOT* INVISIBLE

No, I'm not from Tokyo, Singapore or Saigon.
No, your dogs are safe with me.
No, I don't invade the park for squirrel meat.
No, my peripheral vision is fine.
No, I'm very bad at math.
No, I do not answer to Geisha Girl, China Doll, Suzie Wong,
                mamasan, or gook, Jap or Chink.
No, to us life is not cheap.
I do not know the art of tea, and No,
                I am not grateful for all you've done for me.
                Friends of mine have died from AIDS.
                Another driven mad by P.T.S.D.
                Some of us were murdered, blamed for this economy.
                Another has o.d.'d.
                We've been jailed for mistaken identity.
                Incarcerated because of ancestry,
                And no, I am not the model minority.
No, I am from Stockton, Angel Island, Detroit,
                Waikiki, Los Angeles, Lodi, San Francisco,
                Delano, Chicago, Boston, Tule Lake, New York City,
                Anchorage, Jackson, Phoenix, Raleigh.
And Yes, I am alive because of memory,
                Ancestors who endured adversity,
                all our tongues breaking free,
                the strength of this diversity.
No, we are not Invisible
And Yes, I am from Tokyo, Singapore, Manila, Guam,
                Beijing, Cambodia, Thailand, Vietnam,
                India, Korea, Samoa, Hong Kong, Taiwan.
Yes, this strength like ropes of the sun
again lifts a new morning,
And Yes, we rise as always,
amidst you.

LOOKING FOR AMERICA: FOUND YOU

to The San Francisco Gay Asian Pacific Alliance

I searched for myself and heard you
        talking stories from Hilo rainforests
        Pajaro cauliflower crops,
        Chinatown basements; resurrecting the croon,
        romantic ballads from Karaoke bars,
        the chant of strike lines and uprisings in indigo fields.
I saw myself mirrored
in your pain,
        burying a son before his time,
        gathering up tears on our faces, too dark to be
        loveable in these places.
I meet myself in closets,
        amidst heavy soled shoes,
        semen soiled underwear, erect trouserflies,
        shirtsleeves pinned on hangers.
        You open doors, spilling my secrets into the day.
        We share rituals that save us from madness.
I walk toward myself
        and dance in the circle of your light,
        the warmth of your fire.
        I hear the familiar chant
        and smell the essential same sea.
I press you to my heart and hear the beat
        which is mine.
           Somewhere women are mending their voices,
           somewhere men and women reveal ourselves without fear,
           somewhere children with open faces ask questions.
           Everywhere the old order must listen.
I look for myself
and find you,

        Everywhere,
        singing your song.

PROGENY

The Gulf War was engaged in January, 1991.
Emergency phones were set up at Glide Church,
San Francisco, to provide support and information
about conscription rights to young men and women
of draft age.

Why have they shipped 10,000 body bags to
Saudi Arabia?

She called on the Gulf War Crises Hotline,
I answered, wanting to be useful.
>   Going mad, she said.
>   My tomatoes are rotting in my refrigerator.
>   Such a waste, says she,
>   they've turned off my electricity.
She is furious at inconsiderate people
who steal her SSI checks from her mailbox,
leave their dogs unleashed
to piss on her stairs.
Without the rain the smell rises up
like a disease.
In drought, the ants
are bold in their search for water
and blacken her shelves.
She weeps.
I ask if she is alone.
>   NO I AM NOT ALONE, she screams.
>   A thousand ants seek out my tears.
>   My son is in the Persian Gulf.
>   Unheard of for five weeks.
>   He enlisted when he turned 18.
>   And why not? No jobs here.
>   Enlist. Travel. *Be among a few good men.*
>   Such a waste, said she. Food rotting
>   in a poor refrigerator.

And the people, she rages, drive too fast,
waste gasoline, bullets, burn up rubber,
and why won't it rain?
            She tells me
she lost her husband to Vietnam.
Oh no, she says, not *over there*.
He was not a military casualty
with the telegram and the flag folded
like a pastryturnover,
or his name on that Black Wall, where she
could mourn nationally.
            No, he left into the emptiness of his eyes,
mad nightsweats and finally
to the friendly fire of heroin.
            And my son, she said,
was taught how his father, a patriot,
was a loyal American,
among a few good men,
so my son could follow in his footsteps.
Such a waste, she weeps.
These tomatoes rotting
in my dark, hot refrigerator.

CUMMINGS, GEORGIA

January 25, 1987, Forsythe County, Georgia*

We march,
twenty thousand Americans,
past them lined
beside the road
like pillars of scarfed
and bundled salt.

"Ain't goin to let nobody turn me around,
turn me around . . ."

Faces, too, of America
eyes rimmed red
with hatred,
thin men
in plaid parkas
stocking capped,
lips peeled back, twisted
over stained teeth,
words like bullets:
Nigger.
Jap.
Nigger lovers.
Their women
with blue white necks,
eyes like raisins
whisper through
twisted lips
into the ears of skinny
children whose fingers point
and pull like tiny pistols,
small explosions
gunning from their throats.

The march is long.

Before us
the sky on a thin lip of dawn
is gray, twisting with snow clouds.

> ". . . keeping on a walkin'
> keep on a talkin'
> marchin' up to freedom land . . ."

At our backs
the barrels of little fingers
are pointing,
pointing . . .

The march is long.

---

*In January, 1987, the all white townspeople of Cummings, Georgia, violently ousted a small group of African Americans who had organized to protest Forsythe County's overt racism. No African Americans were allowed to live or work in Forsythe County. As a result of that incident, over 20,000 people from all over the nation, including a planeload of San Franciscans led by Reverend Cecil Williams, gathered in Cummings, Georgia to protest racism and injustice.

WHY IS PREPARING FISH A POLITICAL ACT?

Preparing fish
each Oshogatsu[*]
I buy a gleaming rock cod,
pink, immaculately gutted.
Each year, a respectable fish
that does not satisfy
(hard as I try)
to capture flavors
once tasted.

Grandmother's hands
washing, scaling, cleaning
her fish,
saved each part,
guts, eggs, head.
Her knife, rusted
at the handle screws
ancient as her curled fingers.
Her pot, dented,
darkened, mottled with age
boiled her brew
of shoyu
sweetened with ginger and
herbs she grew
steamed with blood, water.
Nothing wasted.

> Someone once tried to sell her
> a set of aluminum
> pots, smiling too much, called her
> *mamasan.*

Her silence thicker than
steaming shoyu,
whiter than sliced bamboo root
boiled with fish heads.

Preparing fish
is a political act.

RED

For rent.

> I watched
> the chickens circle,
>
> scratching
> out their code.
>
> One of the rules
> of the yard
> was to keep
> the red birds
> away from the white flock.

She,
combed neat,
peeked
from shaded windows.

> The Red
> had flown from her coop
> where she was kept
> apart, now
> surrounded by
> the flock.

She,
sharp eyed
and lidless,
cooed
from the crack
of her door,

There aren't any of you
in this neighborhood.

The flock rushes
and Red
is buried beneath
white feathers flying.
Red's
head bleeding.
Beaks plucking, pecking
crazed by blood.

Old Red. Dead.

Didn't know her place.

GRACIELLA

Graciella's arms,
big like hammocks
swaying mounds of work,
her eyes like moons
moving the waves
of soil   breaking
bursting green leaves
iceberg lettuce.

                    and he watched
                    from the shade of his elm,
                    pleased.

From her body
glistened
wires of water across
her face,
her big arms
cradled the work,
her hands like a weaver,
threading the dirt
to a rich, dark rug
until the sun fell
behind the elm.

                    best damned worker
                    I ever had,
                    good as a dozen wetbacks
                    even with the kid
                    strapped
                    to her back he said, pleased.

From her body
she pushed a child
head swollen
veins rippling
from his hairless skull

                    no work, no pay
                    she doesn't miss a day

they push 'em out like rabbits
he said, pleased.

Into her body
she sucked the sun,
the soil, into her fingers
her pores,
into her nostrils,
her throat
the white chemical dust
sprayed from the cropduster
into her blood
that ran through her child
who died writhing like a hooked worm.

She did not work
that day.

Displeased,
he docked her pay.

He did not offer
her child's grave
to be planted in the shade
of his elm.

1987

JUNGLE ROT AND OPEN ARMS

for a Vietnam Veteran brother, ex-prisoner

Leavenworth
and jungle rot
brought him
back to us
brimming with hate
and disbelief
in love or
sympathy.

his johnnywalker red
eyes
tore at my words
shred my flesh
made naked my
emptiness.

my anger
for the enemy heads
of state
boiled to nothing
             nothing
in the wake
of his rage

jungle rot
had sucked his bones,
his skin fell
like the monsoon
his brain
in a cast in Leavenworth.

In the midst
of genocide

he fell in love
in Vietnam.

"Her hair was
long and dark – like yours"
        he said
"her eyes held the
sixth moon
and when she smiled
the sky opened
and I fell through.

I would crawl
in the tall grasses
to her village

and sleep the war
away with her
like a child on my thighs

I did not know
of the raid

and woke

with her arm
still clasping mine

I could not find
the rest of her

so I buried her arm
and marked my grave."

We sat in a silence
that mocks fools
that lifts us to the final language.

his breath sapped by B-52's
his eyes blinded by the blood of children
his hands bound to bayonets
his soul buried in a shallow grave

i stood amidst
his wreckage
and wept for myself.

so where is my
political education? my
rhetoric answers to everything? my
theory into practice? my
intensification of life in art?

words
are
like
the stone,
the gravemarker
over an arm
in Vietnam.

1977

WE, THE DANGEROUS

I swore
it would not devour me
I swore
it would not humble me
I swore
it would not break me.

      And they commanded we dwell in the desert
      Our children be spawn of barbed wire and barracks

We, closer to the earth,
squat, short thighed,
knowing the dust better.

      And they would have us make the garden
      Rake the grass to soothe their feet

We, akin to the jungle,
plotting with the snake,
tails shedding in civilized America.

      And they would have us skin their fish
      deft hands like blades/sliding back flesh/bloodless

We, who awake in the river
Ocean's child
Whale eater.

      And they would have us strange scented women,
      Round shouldered/strong and yellow/like the moon
      to pull the thread to the cloth
      to loosen their backs massaged in myth

We, who fill the secret bed,
the sweat shops
the launderies.

     And they would dress us in napalm,
     Skin shred to clothe the earth,
     Bodies filling pock marked fields.
     Dead fish bloating our harbors.

We, the dangerous,
Dwelling in the ocean.
Akin to the jungle.
Close to the earth.

     Hiroshima
     Vietnam
     Tule Lake

And yet we were not devoured.
And yet we were not humbled.
And yet we are not broken.

1978

DESERT FLOWERS

Flowers
faded
in the desert wind.
No flowers grow
where dust winds blow
and rain is like
a dry heave moan.

Mama, did you dream about that
beau who would take you
away from it all,
who would show you
in his '41 ford
and tell you how soft
your hands
like the silk kimono
you folded for the wedding?
Make you forget
about That place,
the back bending
wind that fell like a wall,
drowned all your geraniums
and flooded the shed
where you tried to sleep
away hyenas?
And mama,
bending in the candlelight,
after lights out in barracks,
an ageless shadow
grows victory flowers
made from crepe paper,
shaping those petals
like the tears
your eyes bled.
Your fingers

knotted at knuckles
wounded, winding around wire stems
the tiny, sloganed banner:

"america for americans".

Did you dream
of the shiny ford
(only always a dream)
ride your youth
like the wind
in the headless night?

Flowers
2¢ a dozen,
flowers for American Legions
worn like a badge
on america's lapel
made in post-concentration camps
by candlelight.
Flowers
watered
by the spit
of "no japs wanted here",
planted in poverty
of postwar relocations,
plucked by
victory's veterans.

Mama, do you dream
of the wall of wind
that falls
on your limbless desert,
on stems
brimming with petals/crushed
crepepaper
growing

from the crippled
mouth of your hand?

Your tears, mama,
have nourished us.
Your children
like pollen
scatter in the wind.

1978

Bowl of Rage

INSECT COLLECTION

I collected insects
for my biology class
      beetles,
      crickets,
      butterflies,
dropped them into a bottle
of cyanide fumes
and quickly stilled
those beating wings.

                He locked me
                in an airless vault of shame,
                the darkness of closets, barns,
                and muffled bedrooms.
                Kept me in a jar
                of silence,
                the poisons of threat:
                "If you speak of this,
                you will kill your mother."

I pinned dead insects
neatly on paraffin
with gleaming
silver straight needles.

                I think I hear
                butterflies
                scream.
                He peeled back my skin,
                pierced my flesh
                with the dull blades
                of his hands,
                slowly pulled off my wings,
                impaled me, writhing.
                Without swift mercy
                of insecticide
                I suffocated slowly,

swallowing bits of my tongue.
My body,

hollow
as the mute row
of corpses
pinned
to paraffin.

YOU TURNED YOUR HEAD

Mother,
I wanted you to protect me.
I listen for your voice.
You keep changing the subject.
>"A woman must find a man to take care of her,"
>you said.
>"A woman's power is her beauty."
>>Did I know then you lied?
>>Did I smell then your fear?
You tell me how you turned the heads
of all the men at the county fair
in your white dress splashed with red roses.
Even the white men whistled, you said.
>Mother,
>You called me seductress
>when my breasts grew.
>When my period came, you cried.
>You tell me my body is ugly.
>>I listen for your voice.
>>You keep changing the subject.
You tell me with a small smile
how he vowed he would marry you when he first saw you,
your face in the light so beautiful,
your fine pair of legs and small feet
bound in black suede shoes
with sexy slingback straps.
>>"Good riddance," you said, when my father left us,
>>wife/daughter/dead goldfish
>>in shards of glass, gasping for breath.
>>I was not beautiful enough to keep him,
>>you told me, as I waited for his return,
>>my heart underwater,
>>sinking in silence.
When you brought home your new husband,
you thought he would never look at another.

He was dazzled by the curve of your waist,
his hands on your back, pressing/pressing as you
dipped in the swing of his arm.
                Mother, you made me believe
                beauty was power.
Where was your power
when his hands like crowbars
spread my thighs
and I became a slab of concrete
beneath the jackhammer of his need?
                I wanted you to save me.
                You turned your head.
The farm harvests loneliness. It stretches
in silence like endless furrows,
and steaming piles of chicken manure, horse dung.
                Mother, I listen for your voice.
                I am eight years old.
You send me to keep him company
in the rain that is gray.
I cannot walk in the river of mud and manure
that rises above my waist.
                You keep changing the subject.
He carried me out to the pasture in the rain,
He reached into my underpants and held me upside down
by my ankles and said if I screamed
he would drop me under the shit until my mouth,
my nose would fill with it, and I
would never speak again.
                Mother, I wanted you to save me.
                You turned your head.
        He says if I tell, you will die, Mother.
I sever my self from my body.
My tongue in a glass bowl, underwater.

I want to hear your comfort,
paste your voice to my skin
like velvet China nights.
Kiss the power of your beautiful face.
I wanted you to love me.

Mother. You turned your head.

THE ABORTION

You said
he wanted to abort
me.

You didn't think he noticed
the swell of your belly,
the cessation of your
womanblood,
you, untouched as silent
fever.

It runs in our veins,
you said,
this curse of bearing females.

> Your mother suffered with nine,
>> one son born dead.
>> How the fields shook that day
>> hungry for seed, you said.
>> Incense smothered at the altar,
>> salt poured at the doorstep
>> to keep away bad luck dissolved by sudden rain.
>> So many prayers
>> unheard.
>> Women have no destiny, only luck.
>> The male child is dead.
>> And the future cries.

The tree bark outside
the hospital
was the color of your face
in the killing room
as they scraped me from your womb
carefully with razor precision.
    Now you keep me

in a glass jar
soaked in vinegar
next to the pickled scallions
and wrinkled dried plums.
 The wind outside
strays in gingko leaves,
dipping like bells.
The moon glazes the hill.
 Over steaming rice,
he dips me in ginger and shoyu,
bites off the toes
crunchy like kazunoko – fish eggs
cut from the belly of herring.
 He slurps his cha
sloshing his throat to clear
bits of me
from his teeth.
 Swallows.

 Satisfied.
He lights a cigarette.

BOWL OF RAGE

What do I do with these resentments?

> The unspoken seethings?
> the betrayals,
> forcible entries,
> violations?

>> *I know the rage comes from somewhere as deep and far as*
>> *childhood. I don't want to be rational.*
>> *I hear the shhh shhh of his slippers,*
>> *entering my small door.*
>> *Rage would seep into that little hole made*
>> *by his fingers, slip inside like a worm.*
>> *He whispers, shhh, don't tell*
>> *and I spoil from my core, like infested apples.*
>> *My surface is smooth, placid. Appetizing.*

What do I do with these resentments?

> The unspoken seethings?
> The presumption of superiority,
> flattery without feeling,
> manipulation, humiliation,
> racism?

>> *I know the rage comes from history. Don't ask*
>> *me to be logical.*
>> *I can't forget the tall white man with large hands*
>> *over my mother's breasts. Small melons, he called them,*
>> *her arms wrapped behind her, weaponless, as he cooed,*
>> *shhh shhh with the pocketing of his papers,*
>> *unpaid bills he waved to show his power.*

What do I do with these resentments?

> Growing up female in the shadow of male ness?
> The double standard,
> second classness,
> imprinted self sabotage,
> womanfighting – the she who calls our home,
> treats me like the maid,
> the smirk, catty line,

the omissions, small insults like razor nicks
that bleed too much.

> *I know the rage comes from tradition.*
> *I can't be reasonable.*
> *Man is the tree where birds nest,*
> *the horizon where the sun sets,*
> *centerstage where all eyes rest.*

What do I do with these resentments?

> The unspoken seethings?
> The self we are taught to hate in women,
> the weakness and self-sacrifice,
> the silence of shame,
> the not-enoughness,
> the motherness of our suffering?

> Do I kill them with the heel
> of my shoe, like cockroaches,
> to be scraped and flushed down my toilet?

> Do I keep these words between my teeth,
> allow them to become caries
> rotting to the final nerve,
> novocained with lies?

> Do I pick them, one by one,
> like strawberries, sugar them,
> drench them in cream,
> crush them behind my lips,
> chew,
> swallow?
> vomit?

> Or do I gather them in a bowl,
> polish, display them
> like fruit,

and as women learn to master well,
tempt him
to eat?

WHERE BODIES ARE BURIED

A cycle for the circle of Women in Recovery,
Glide Church, San Francisco, 1993

Winter, 1990

We gather in this circle,
we women who have huddled
within ourselves too long,
we with shovels hewn
from our tongues, excavate into the caves
of our pain.
       I told you,
Jeannine, who smells of autumn,
rain clean, spice fragrant,
about the autumn in Hartford.
Leaves are rust,
red/orange, aflame in the morning
as I jog,
the man with whiteblond hair and worker's
bulging arms, yells from his truck,
              what are you? where are you from?
There is always danger, I tell
you who know about our vulnerability,
about men who want to hurt us.
            They are incomplete, broken in places
            they want to hide. They carry weapons
            to imitate body parts,
            and damage things, throw us against walls,
            then paste our pieces
            onto their wounds.
The air is white,
like ice in my lungs. I am running, faster,
not sure footed on this ground,
and remember the sacrificial Japanese
manufactured cars bashed in Detroit,

burning like epitaphs on the roadsides
of America.

      I yell to him in my best
San Francisco accent
that we are sure to win the Superbowl.
He smiles, returning the long object to his truck.

                I wonder where the bodies are
                buried.

Autumn, 1942

They met before dawn
under the barrack,
behind barbed wire.
He laid the blanket in the crawlspace
and began to peel her buttons one by one,
her small moon breasts soft
in his hands.
She smiles into his warm chest
as he slides her skirt up.

                And then, laughter like nails,
                lights flashing like knives,
                army boots kicking dust into their faces,
                soldiers' shouts: *japs fuck sideways.*

They slither out like lizards
from under the barrack, arms outstretched.
She wriggles like an overturned beetle,
as they roll her onto her back,
and the cold steel barrel of the rifle
rips open her skirt.

                After the war,
                after they were released from camp,[1]
                it is said he never married.
                Buried in a bottle
                somewhere in Gilroy.

---

[1]During World War II, over 110,000 Americans of Japanese ancestry were unjustly incarcerated in ten concentration camps throughout America. In 1987, President Ronald Reagan signed the Redress Bill granting reparations to those Japanese Americans who were interned.

Winter, 1989

"What are you? When did you arrive?
Where did you learn to speak English so well?"

"You people
aren't like *Them*.
You're clean, hard working,
know when to keep quiet."

"You oriental girls are soooo sexy,
especially now with all these raving
feminists
running around . . ."

"The best way to handle the trade imbalance,"
suggests a major automobile manufacturing executive,
"would be to charter the Enola Gay. Get it?
The plane that dropped The Bomb . . . hahahahaha . . ."

Summer, 1945

All the bodies
buried
beneath a mushroom
cloud.

A young woman's
hair,
thick and long
to her waist,
falls out
in her comb.
Black rain
pours over Hiroshima,
lifeless
as falling
hair.

Summer, 1954

Where is home?
A quail flutters from the tall grass
where her chicks are hidden.
She will sacrifice herself,
distract danger, feign crippledness
to protect her young.
       Sparrows scream, beat wings,
peck at mockingbirds trying to kidnap her eggs.
       Mother hens will attack even humans
when close to hatching chicks.
       Uncle Harry
they told me to call him.
Pays for his keep.
Chick sexer Harry, on his off season
comes to stay at our house.
       Chick sexers make a lot of money,
his hands are like a piano player or surgeon,
insured.
His fingers are always rubbing, his nails manicured.
He says he can feel the miniature sex of the rooster,
sexing out the female chicks.
The men marvel.
Harry's hair is wavy, slicked back
dripping with pomade.
His eyes are slitted like a bat's.
When I told Harry to keep his sensitive
hands off of me, he told my mother
I was rude, and perhaps he should find
a rooming house in town.
My mother said it was my fault if we starved
that winter. Uncle Harry
paid well for his room and board
and lets us drive his Cadillac.
It should not be so hard to be
polite.

Spring, 1992

In the circle,
Ntombi asked,
     "Why me?"
     When you were a child and shame
     came like a thief,
     stole you out of your body.
In the darkness of why,
in the cages of why me?
in the corners where girl bodies
were tossed like soiled cloth,
we met.
Pummeled and propped up
like broken furniture,
we knew one another by our bruises,
discovered that we counted the same stars
sang the same rituals,
whispered the same prayers
     nonononot tonight.
Why you? Why me?
appointed to this circle
to pull the children out of
dark corners. Why?

     Perhaps you recognise her?
She kept repeating herself,
insane, they diagnosed her.
     one   two   buckle my shoe
     three   four   lock my door.
perhaps you recognise her.
She is considered dangerous
so they gagged her
kept her in a room without windows.
     five   six   pull out your stick
     seven   eight   shut the gate

She pleaded to be set free
but they called her crazy.
Perhaps you recognise her?
      She keeps wringing her hands,
      pulling her hair, seeing racists at her door,
      peeling her lip, eating, vomiting, bingeing,
      drinking, smoking, shooting up, popping, having sex,
      watching t.v., gambling, stealing, overspending,
      hustling, talking
      nine   ten   rape me again
      don't rape me again   *daddy*.
Perhaps you recognise . . .

Summer, 1955

I washed my hair
in the outdoor garage basin
so I wouldn't stop up the plumbing.
I'm soap blinded,
groping for rinsewater.
Harry with his hard-on is rubbing,
rubbing against me.
He pulls the wings off big, dusty gray
moths with antennas like horns.
His chick sexer fingers on my puberty breasts.
He whispers,
         be polite
or he will stuff the fat bodies of moths
into my ears, make them crawl between
my lips
and they will deposit their eggs
in my throat, spin my face
into their nest
         my face, a helpless
         cloth,
         eaten by moths.
In my dreams, I prepare dinner
for Harry.

I take the knife
my mother uses to cut
vegetables and de-bone fish.
I scale the nerve endings
from his sensitive fingers,
show him the art of slicing
that my mother,
          who cuts so fast you can't see her hands,
has taught me,
and ever so politely,
I will serve him cucumber
for salad.

1963–1993

Cecil:
          you built a church
          where this circle could abide
          without fear or shame,
          without betrayal.
                    You told us all
          to come and be,
          help bring together our missing
          parts. Come
          to sing,   to feast.
          You prepared a table for women:
                    she who danced naked, on her way to the asylum,
                    she who discarded her children for drugs,
                    she who loved her bruises like kisses,
                    the woman who cut out her tongue.
                    Come, you said, to rest,
          take comfort, dress
          our throats with power.
                    Here I discovered
          myself in the women you loved.
                    You assigned us
                    to listen like a miracle
                    so I may reclaim
                    the song which is mine.

Summer, 1991 – In the Mirror

M. told me:

> You made your body into a box,
> boarded and still
> so he would not rape your baby sister
> who lay sleeping next to you.
> You whimper
> and he drives the nail into your tongue.
>> You think you see your mother
>> dressed in white, floating like mist,
>> smelling of gardenias and milk,
>> taking you out of the box and she bathes
>> you in fragrant oils.
> She sets a bowl before you.
> You crawl to it, scooping bits of bread
> soaked in broth with your fingers.
> As you eat, the belt slaps against your buttocks.

Welts rise,
frothing immediately red.
You twist and soil yourself
as you swing again the belt
and again until you are a swollen
red bead rolling from your tongue.
Your baby sister licks your lips.
She gets fat.

>> Where is mother?
>> You say,
>> that will teach her, my girl,
>> o child in me,
>> to talk, to tell,
>> to dare to succeed.
>> Now will I nail the coffin shut
>> or must I?

> I know little
> I scarcely   see

fear eats my eyelids
like moths,
afraid of who
she is.
At the stone
where the dust covers names,
we gather in a circle.
We have begun
to know one another
> when the day opens like morning glories,
> when the wind moves our words,
> when rain
> smells like hope.
We know
in our hunger
in our essential feeding of one another,
it matters not
whose name
is carved upon the face of rock.

Summer, 1957

Harry had stayed four off-seasons,
each lasting three months.
During those times,
I learned to wash my hair in daylight
when sun would glint like blades
through the slitted roof.
At night I slept
beneath a stone.
Harry met a hairdresser
who had a loud voice and pimples,
said she loved his sensitive hands
that played her like a keyboard.
He called her "his chick",
and though she wasn't as young
as he liked, she had great breasts,
and manicured his nails.

Summer, 1948

Femicide.
She deserved to die, her husband said,
dragging her by her hair,
clumps scattered in the rug.
She is twisting like a headless chicken.
He caught her behind the sofa
on the floor with the greasy faced
chinaman, he called him,
that bony hairless horny yellow shit
who propelled his skinny yellow sperm into her.
He left.
And she, disgraced by divorce,
was quietly buried.
Not spoken of again.

   She almost died, was not the same
after that beating.
She walked with a quiver,
peed on the sofa as if to mark
territory.
She looked like a bruise with a thin veil
of skin covering her.
The chinaman stayed with her,
would carry her to their bedroom
over his bony back,
bathed her like a child
and cooed to her in Cantonese
because it made her smile
through her broken teeth.

Spring, 1992

Edna Lois
said that once she found her truth,
she had no more to lose.

   You can live with what you can carry,
your name, your self, your soul,
and pay your own way.

I tell you that we have paid
sufficiently,
for all the cousins, priests, bosses, fathers,
uncle Harrys . . .
We paid through our shame and bruises,
our stitched lips and sacrificed thighs,
our veins pumped with heroin, crack.
We paid each time we laid underneath them,
and choked back the sperm and screams.
We paid enough
      so now you can say,
          "Every time I break my silence
          I earn my freedom."

Edna Lois.
You picked up your face
and put it on.
Your eyes,
clear like a mirror,
your cheeks, full and blushed,
each line,
each curve defined
by the truth.
      Look. See.
      Our beauty.

Autumn 1992

Femicide prevention.
      Jeannine, you told me about the women
who save our lives
because they dare to go mad
and tell everything.
      We pull them from bags and purses
and dress them in roses and old lace handkerchiefs.
We carry them to the light
over our bony backs, and they,
drawn up to full height,

hold their white hankies to their lips
and delicately, eloquently
tell us how to survive.
She sings about her youth,
her dreams,
with infinite compassion, she touches
our bruises, too.
She tells us how she endured, how to protect
chicks from snakes and mockingbirds
by distracting hunters, by acting crippled,
and she succeeded.
Now as we give her light,
listen to her voice, moths circling,
she is not afraid.
   She washes in the sound
of her words
as she tells us
where
   the bodies
   are buried.
At the stone
each name
is revealed.
   We have begun
   to know one another.
   The stone is lifted.
A child emerges,
her small hands grasp roses.
We feed her petals.
Today,
she blooms
within
our
bodies.

WITHOUT TONGUE

The sun stood among corn, dead in summer.
Dust whirlwinding off dry fields.
He had awoken her for the last time,
burying his head into her shoulder, clawing
open her thighs like the wide branches of stone pine.
She lay, passive, as always. Breathless. Without tongue,
a dead boat on the bottom of the sea,
a wingless beetle waiting for descending shoe.
She dresses. Walks to the meadow shaded
with hawthorne, oak, white birch.
She lifts the rock where she had buried the knife,
afraid she would use it to kill her father.
Her tongue tastes its cold steel edge,
shrill like blood.
She returns to her kitchen, water steaming
in the kettle. Prepares tea
with leaves of shiso no ha, soaked in kyoto plum
and salt. Dried. Sweet bitterness on her tongue.
Chinese flowers bloom in her throat.
She cleans the blade and returns it to the drawer.

After forty years of silence
about the experience of Japanese
Americans in World War II concentration
camps, my mother testified before the
Commission on Wartime Relocation and
Internment of Japanese American
Civilians in 1981.

BREAKING SILENCE

For my mother

There are miracles that happen
she said.
From the silences
in the glass caves of our ears,
from the crippled tongue,
from the mute, wet eyelash,
testimonies waiting like winter.
    We were told
that silence was better
golden like our skin,
        useful like
go quietly,
        easier like
don't make waves,
        expedient like
horsestalls and deserts.

            "Mr. Commissioner . . .
            . . . the U.S. Army Signal Corps confiscated
            our property . . . it was subjected to
            vandalism and ravage. All improvements
            we had made before our incarceration
            was stolen or destroyed . . .

I was coerced into signing documents
giving you authority to take . . ."
to take
to take.

My mother,
soft as tallow,
words peeling from her
like slivers of yellow flame.
Her testimony,
a vat of boiling water
surging through the coldest
bluest vein.
        She had come to her land
as shovel, hoe and sickle searing
reed and rock and dead brush,
labored to sinew the ground
to soften gardens pregnant with seed
awaiting each silent morning
birthing
fields of flowers,
mustard greens and tomatoes
throbbing like the sea.
        And then
All was hushed for announcements:
        "Take only what you can carry . . ."
We were made to believe our faces
betrayed us.
Our bodies were loud
with yellow screaming flesh
needing to be silenced
behind barbed wire.

        "Mr. Commissioner . . .
        . . . it seems we were singled out
        from others who were under suspicion.
        Our neighbors were of German and

Italian descent, some of whom were
not citizens . . . It seems we were
singled out . . ."

She had worn her work
like lemon leaves,
shining in her sweat,
driven by her dreams that honed
the blade of her plow.
The land she built
like hope
grew quietly
irises, roses, sweet peas
opening, opening.
    And then
all was hushed for announcements:
    ". . . to be incarcerated for your own good"
The sounds of her work
bolted in barracks . . .
silenced.

        Mr. Commissioner . . .
        So when you tell me I must limit
        testimony,
        when you tell me my time is up,
        I tell you this:
        Pride has kept my lips
        pinned by nails
        my rage coffined.
        But I exhume my past
        to claim this time.
        My youth is buried in Rohwer,
        Obachan's ghost visits Amache Gate.
        My niece haunts Tule Lake.
        Words are better than tears,
        so I spill them.
        I kill this,
        the silence . . .

There are miracles that happen
she said,
and everything is made visible.
        We see the cracks and fissures in our soil:
We speak of suicides and intimacies,
of longings lush like wet furrows,
of oceans bearing us toward imagined riches,
of burning humiliations and
crimes by the government.
Of self hate and of love that breaks
through silences.
        We are lightning and justice.
        Our souls become transparent like glass
revealing tears for war-dead sons
red ashes of Hiroshima
jagged wounds from barbed wire.
        We must recognize ourselves at last.
        We are a rainforest of color
and noise.
        We hear everything.
        We are unafraid.

                Our language is beautiful.

*(Quoted excerpts from my mother's testimony, modified
with her permission)*

1982

PRISONS OF SILENCE

(Performed by the Asian American Dance
Collective, 1983 Repertory Concert)

1.

The strongest prisons are built
with walls of silence.

2.

Morning light falls between us
like a wall.
We have laid beside each other
as we have for years.
Before the war, when life
would clamor through our windows,
we woke joyfully to the work.

I keep those moments
like a living silent seed.

After day's work, I would
smell the damp soil in his hands,
his hands that felt the outlines
of my body in the velvet
night of summers.

I hold his warm hands to this
cold wall of flesh
as I have for years.

3.

Jap!
Filthy Jap!

Who lives within me?

Abandoned homes, confiscated land,
loyalty oaths, barbed wire prisons
in a strange wasteland.

Go home, Jap!
Where is home?

A country of betrayal.
No one speaks to us.

We would not speak to each other.

We were accused.

Hands in our hair,
hands that spread our legs
and searched our thighs for secret
weapons.
hands that knit barbed wire
to cripple our flight.

Giant hot hands flung me,
fluttering, speechless into
barbed wire, thorns in a broken wing.

The strongest prisons are built
with walls of silence.

4.

I watched him depart that day
from the tedious wall of wire,
the humps of barracks,
handsome in his uniform.

I would look each day for letters
from a wall of time,
waiting for approach of my deliverance
from a wall of dust.

I do not remember
reading about his death
only the wall of wind
that encased me, as I turned my head.

5.

U.S. Japs hailed as heroes!

I do not know the face of this country
it is inhabited by strangers
who call me obscene names.

Jap. Go home.
Where is home?

I am alone wandering
in this desert.

Where is home?
Who lives within me?

A stranger with knife in her tongue
and broken wing,
mad from separations and losses cruel
as hunger.

Walls suffocate her as a tomb,
encasing history.

6.

I have kept myself contained
within these walls shaped to my body
and buried my rage.

I rebuilt my life
like a wall, unquestioning.
Obeyed their laws . . . their laws.

7.

All persons of Japanese ancestry
filthy jap.
Both alien and non-alien
japs are enemy aliens.
To be incarcerated
for their own good
A military necessity
The army to handle only the japs.
Where is home?
A country of betrayal.

8.

This wall of silence crumbles
from the bigness of their crimes.
This silent wall
crushed by living memory.

He awakens from the tomb
I have made for myself
and unearths my rage.

I must speak.

9.

He faces me in this small
room of myself.
I find the windows
where light escapes.

From this cell of history
this mute grave,
we birth our rage.

We heal our tongues.

We listen to ourselves

      Korematsu, Hirabayashi, Yasui.

We ignite the syllables of our names.

We give testimony.

We hear the bigness of our sounds freed
like many clapping hands,
thundering for reparations.

We give testimony.

Our noise is dangerous.

10.

We beat our hands
like wings healed.

We soar
from these walls of silence.

FOR MY FATHER

He came over the ocean
carrying Mt. Fuji
on his back/Tule Lake* on his
chest
hacked through the brush
of deserts
and made them grow
strawberries

> we stole berries
> from the stem
> we could not afford them
> for breakfast

his eyes held
nothing
as he whipped us
for stealing.

the desert had dried
his soul.

wordless
he sold
the rich,
full berries
to hakujines
whose children
pointed at our eyes

> they ate fresh
> strawberries
> with cream.

Father,
I wanted to scream
at your silence.
Your strength
was a stranger
I could never touch.

iron
in your eyes
to shield
the pain
to shield desert-like wind
from patches
of strawberries
grown
from
tears.

1978

*Tule Lake Camp, located in a barren desert area of California, was designated of the ten American concentration camps as the 'segregation center' for 'dissident' Japanese Americans.

HOSPITALS ARE TO DIE IN

They finally
had to take obachan
she was dying

       hospitals
       takai
            takai
       she whispered

but she is dying

when they carried her
body
barely breathing,
they were carrying my soul
wrapped in the thin sheath
of her skin.

The ambulance attendants
rushed from their
coffee break
irritated,
dropped her on the
stretcher
and bumped her
against the door
violating her sleep.

She wanted to stay
die in the house
that was like a body
wrapping her
in smells she knew
breathing memories
for her.

In the corners
of her closed eyes
silent tears brimming
protesting
not the hospital

       cold
       white
       expensive

the attendants swore
as they slung
the stretcher

complaining
about the high cost of living.

One said
he had to buy a
side of beef
to hang in his freezer.

       it's cheaper that way.

1978

". . . IF YOU DON'T WANT TO BELIEVE IT . . ."

Coffee steaming,
my daughter asleep
safely in the morning.
There are trees outside
that bloom here.
Wind brushes the begonias
dusting mist from
their eyes.
The sun slides
through my blinds
like razors.

Dateline, Johannesburg.
Soldier shoots a nine year old
black child in Soweto.
He thought he was shooting a dog.

A state of emergency.
Toaster burns out,
refrigerator broken,
these gadgets tied to my hands
not to comprehend
wholesale detention, slaughter.
The easy distraction of the blender,
tending of gardens.

A black child
dead.

Newsprint flickers
over the sea, the mountains,
the plains of drying bones,
blood flecked corrugated
iron fences.

A black child is dead.
He thought it was a dog.

Dead black child.
Lucifer's smile,
like dead light
with all the care of diamonds
wrapped to our fingers.

Dead black child
mistaken for a dog.
The official response:
". . . if you don't want to believe it,
you don't have to."

His smile glinting like
the cold white stones in his mines.

(*Quote from South African Government spokesman,*
San Francisco Chronicle, June 21, 1986.)

1986

Woman With
Straight Back

WOMAN WITH STRAIGHT BACK

Inspired by my Mother who said upon
the signing of the Redress Bill in August, 1987:
"We deserve it. Damn it. And I'll stay
alive to collect so they don't dare do
it again . . ."

For Sandy Mori and Emma Gee

"I am this stone,"
she says . . . "smooth, oval.
My memory is a chisel
from which I shape myself."

> The stone hung at her chest
> tied by the thinnest chain,
> invisible around her neck.
> She wore it close
> to her skin, like normal garment.
> The weight caused her
> to straighten her back,
> chin high,
> rising against it.

"To understand,
you must contemplate pride,"
she said.

> Graystone flecked with white,
> granite, touchstone.

Not the insolence of vanity
or conceit . . .

> Cobble, dolomite,
> hedge-rose sand,
> mirror stones the pale shade
> of shame.

It is called "face" – controlled
emotion, self-consequence,
quiet dignity.

She pulls against
the growing weight,
sand-grain-on-grain
like each moment dropped
in the mute well of memory:
The work wore her young
shoulders sore, building the farm,
plowing new life, she pregnant with hope
and first child.
The sacks of seed were counted
        like coins,
        memory:
the sudden invasions by government men
who slit the sacks
to pour into their bins,
let the apples rot
and tomatoes burst
as they scraped away the land;
The horse stalls in Stockton
that steamed with manure
where she, "detained", slept;
The trains with shadedrawn windows
taking only what she could carry;
The vomiting,
The endless dark ride
to Arkansas swamps
and one room barracks;
The open toilets for women
who hid their shame, covered their heads
with brown paper bags.
        Carefully, she chisels
        a woman's mouth
        in the stone.
"I delivered mail in camp.
The letters weighed
like slabstone
to the old couple whose five sons

enlisted in the U.S. army
to prove they were loyal Americans.
All five were killed
in combat.
The mail. Heavier
than weapons.
To the Issei
whose brother was lost
whose country was lost
in the Hiroshima bombing.
He cursed, hurling
a fistful of dirt at me
for bringing the news."

> *Obsidian, serpentine,*
> *sandstone.*
> *Today the Redress Bill*
> *is signed.*

She removes the stone
from her neck,
her body lighter
than water.

> *Carefully with the chisel*
> *of her tongue*
> *she shapes the curve of*
> *her throat.*

To understand,
contemplate pride.
"Yes.
I will take the Reparations.
I deserve it.
It's not the amount.
No monetary measure can price
injustice and loss and humiliation,
the years of 'face' silent as stone.
But if it will make them think
before they do it again
to anyone else,

I'll stay alive to exact the apology
as physical as a gash
across the face of their national budget."
Memory is the chiseled shape
of a woman with straight back,
holding a rock the size
of an apology.
She will stand
chin high,
at the doorway of history.
     AND NO,
     WE,
     NONE WILL GO INTO
     THOSE CAMPS AGAIN.

CRY

For the ten infants buried at Tule
Lake who died during the
incarceration of Japanese
Americans during WW II and to
those artists and activists in the
Northwest Asian Communities
who in 1990 erected new gravestones to
keep their memory alive.

There are knives in the child's crib.
Blades of desert wind
cut the cord from its mother's
womb,
a chain of dust
around its throat.
Matsubara Baby, Tetsuno Kiyono,
Yamamoto Baby.
When the stone speaks
we will not forget
Okada Baby, Hirao Dick Nishizaki.
Perhaps in easier times
you would have lived.
Infants buried at Tule Lake.
Yamamuro Baby, George Uyeda,
Kazuo Harry Nishizaki, Loni Miyoko Toriumi,
Seki Baby.
Peonies plucked
by cruel weather, crushed into the sand,
suffocated in a jar with tight lid.

>   *Your cry*
>   *would have made*
>   *the pain go away.*
>   *I could have soothed*
>   *with lullaby*
>>   *hush little baby and when you wake*
>>   *your mother will feed you omame*

> *sleep little one and fret no more*
> *your daddy's home from the war.*

Government made gravemarker,
makeshift, crumbling –
a cruel history,
all Japs are enemy aliens.
Infants?
buried
in concentration camps.
Something withers
starved of justice.

> *There is no meat or fish or milk*
> *rationed to rutabagas and potatoes,*
> *infirmaries smell of death.*
> *My breasts are dried*
> *and flat*
> *like this cracked earth*
> *beneath the barracks.*
> *The hot wind creeps*
> *into my womb*
> *and takes your breath.*
> *The hot, barren desert wind*
> *slices your hearts*
> *severs your throats*
> *before you could cry*
> *or blossom.*

Cry.

We will
> *carry you beyond these gates*
> *and barbed wire that encage us.*
run to the place
of live flowers,
walk the earth
with you to the ocean with its eternal
life, roaring for freedom,

comb your hair black like kelp
tied with bright red ribbons,
tell you about destinies that lie
before you vast as the orange horizon
> *your arms*
> *reach like wings of astronauts,*
> *discoverers, peacemakers,*
> *singers, poets*
> *with breath and story.*

We listen
as the wind with tongues
carves your names into stone

> *hush little baby and when you wake*

We plant you
beneath gingko and pine,
fragrant cherry, quince,
where tall grasses
grow in a mist
that comes from the sea.
> *Perpetual blooms*
> *will spring forth*
> *to remind us*
> *that you were born*
> *to be reborn*

and our lips
will whisper lullabyes

> *sleep little one and fret no more.*

In the middle
of the desert
protected from harsh wind
a new stone with mouth

cries.

The war in urban America most tragically affects the children. Over 600,000 refugees fled by sea after the fall of South Vietnam in 1975. By 1981, more than 450,000 refugees had resettled in the United States. There are currently 12,000 Indochinese immigrants residing in San Francisco's Tenderloin neighborhood alone, where they live in low cost housing units neglected by slumlords. A Vietnamese child was found murdered in an elevator of one of these tenements.

ORCHID DAUGHTER

My girl, you were always independent.
My orchid child, wildly beautiful
chasing ducks even before you could walk,
your thick black hair jumping alive in the breeze.

    I shaved your head
to disguise you as a boy, make you ugly
to Thai pirates who preyed on small refugee boats
seeking asylum.

    They would get top price for you
in Malaysian slave markets.

    As Ben Hai River floats us gently away
from the smoking grasses, the charred bamboo gardens
of our town, I whisper to you: Forget Vietnam.

    My daughter, I did not know
as we navigated the treacherous sea,
seeking peace,
that we would trade one war for hell.
In a city named for a Saint of Peace,
a hotel that looked firebombed was all we could afford,
one room with barely a kitchen for five of us.
I remember we rejoiced the luxury of an elevator.

    You, my independent one,
learned too quickly the lessons of these streets,
dodging drunks and nodding men with needles
in their hands.

My sweet smiled child,
at eight years old
what a comfort you were to me,
learning English so you could shop,
speak for me, navigate these dark seas of concrete.
No trees can live in this filth and soot,
the rotten smell of sweat and whisky.
        My beloved girl,
I do not remember how they said
they found you in the elevator,
legs bloodied, your black hair dead and matted,
your neck like the tender stalk of a flower,
snapped, broken.
        My Orchid Daughter,
I cannot plant new seeds
in these concrete streets.
There is no sunlight, no soil,
        Only the rain that falls
        from my face,
        like the monsoons of the Mekong
        without pause,
        without mercy . . .

WITHOUT COMFORT

Written for Amonita Balajadia on her visit
to San Francisco from the Philippines in
November, 1993, speaking for the
Comfort Women's Movement for
Restitution. Over 200,000 Asian women
were kidnapped and raped, used as sex
slaves by Japanese and other
imperialist armies during World War II.

I hear the story of girls/women
whose bones are wrung from their flesh
and carved for the comfort of brutal men
who make wars.

     I dream of you, Amonita Balajadia,
of girls stolen and enslaved,
pressed into the flesh of trees,
into fragments of rock.

     The rivers turn red from sorrows,
fish weep, small animals who drink of it scream.
The birds take the cries to the air.
Groans are heard from the throat of mountains.

     I think of my daughter
       and the daughters of the world.
The sky's face awakens.
Lightning sparks her lips.
Trees stand up like women.
They have drunk too many tears.
Rocks cleave open, and bleed.
Our skirts whirl in fury.
Our ears catch the screams of girls,
push them into the muscles of our jaws, into the sinews
of our shoulders,
our arms,
into our fingers that squeeze
bullets from our tongues.

They hear. All hear.
The men who assault women hear:
Not tonight.
Our children will not comfort soldiers this night.
Not any night.

JANE

"I'm fine now that I know I have cancer.
At least my depression has now something
real to define it . . ."

Jane

Jane
rocking in her bosom
with laughter,
that wide opened mouthed,
head back, breath bucking
laugh,
catches us in its gust,
whirls our limbs akimbo,
our joy cycloning
around our frailties, our sicknesses.
And we laugh
at the twinkies, potato chips, fudge,
bean pie, vanilla ice cream and oreos binge,
because our bodies,
layered with self loathing,
leap into the mirror
to tickle us.
We laugh
over daughters who are too much
like ourselves,
choosing brutish men, cold men who with
finger snapping ease
can expunge us mothers into oblivion. . . .
before we can say, "d d d don't . . ."
We laugh
over those women
so in denial, so envious
that they would skingraft for penile implants
in their need to screw other women
behind their backs,

while whispering "I Love You" to our faces,
because she is us, who we hate
in ourselves, and can't resist. That is so funny.

     Jane
cradles in her bosom
her depression
which is like the weather,
unpredictable, persistent.
But she laughs
her heart filling/face stretching/
life-making/joy jumping/nothing matters/
but the moment's
laughter   spilling
into that bosom which is dwindling
from lumpectomies
diagnosed malignant.

     And life,
open mouthed,
lipstick clear,
breath pirouetted life,
makes us laugh
so hard

we cry.

GENERATIONS OF WOMEN

I

She rests,
rocking to ritual,
the same sun fades
the same blue dress
covering her knees
turned inward
from weariness.
The day is like the work
she shoulders,
sacks of meal, corn, barley.
But her sorrow wears
like steady rain.
She buried him yesterday.
Incense still gathered
in her knuckles knotted
from the rubbings
the massage with nameless
oils, on his swollen gouted feet,
his steel girded back,
muscled from carrying calves,
turning brutal rock,
building fields of promises,
gardens alive with camellias,
peaches, clover.

Time has sucked my body.
He is buried
in his one black suit
we kept in mothballs
for that day.
I want to lay next to him
in my gold threaded wedding
kimono, grandly purple

with white cranes in flight,
drape my bones with
wisteria.
I want to shed the century
of incense resting in my pores
like sweat or dirt.
I want to fly with the birds
in this eternal silk,
heading sunward
for warm matings.
I want this soil
that wraps him
to sleep in the smell
of my work.

Obachan
walked to the store
wearing respectable
shoes, leather
hard like a wall
against her sole.
She carefully fingered her coins
in the pocket of her thinning
blue dress,
saved for sugar, salt and yellow onions.
The clerk's single syllable spit
out a white wall –
JAP.
She turned to the door
with shopping bag empty as the sound
of her feet in
respectable shoes.
There are no tears
for moments as these.

II

Her body speaks,
arms long,
thin as a mantis.

I am afraid
to leave this room
of myself, imprisoned
by walls of cloth.
Only the man clocks
my moments,
as he fingers the
corners of my fabric,
empty buttonholes,
my muslin,
sandy as a desert.
I wait.
I wait for his presence,
my flesh like
sheets drying in the wind.
I wait,
weaving chains of flowers
to scent my hands,
color my skin,
mourn my loss.
I wait
for him to open
the bloom
hidden in the folds
of flannel.
I do not remember
being beautiful or proud.

Some losses
can't be counted:
departures to desert camps

and barracks,
men leaving to separate
camps or wars
and finally to houses
walled white full with women
in silk dresses,
wilted flowers and rhinestones
around their necks,
fast drinking, quick joking
women with red lipstick
sleek
and slippery as satin.
Her thin arms
chained by wringing
and worry
and barbed wire
slashing her youth,
her neck bowed to history
and past pain that haunts
her like a slain woman-child.

> *I watched as they*
> *let her die – seventh sister*
> *born like a blue fish into*
> *that dry orange day.*
> *No more women, they prayed,*
> *a son. A son to carry on the name.*

Some losses can't be counted:
abandonments left her
frightened, hungry,
made her count the grains
of rice,
wrinkles in her cheek,
pieces of rock in the desert
sand, shadows of guardtower
soldiers, mornings without

waking men,
the syllables of her name.
Some imprisonments are permanent:
white walls encaged her
with a single syllable:
JAP.
Her lips puckered
from humiliations
that made her feel like mildewed cloth,
smelling with neglect.
Her body a room
helpless to the exit of men.
The day he left her for the
red-lipped woman,
she, damp, wringing,
stood between desert camps
and bedrooms,
brooding for unburied female infants,
her thin arms dripping chains
of flowers
weighted with tears.

III

Two generations
spit me out
like phlegm,
uncooked rice
one syllable words,
a woman foetus.
There are few places
that are mine.
I claim them,
this ground,
this silent piece of sky

where embroidered cranes keep vigil,
this purple silk smelling of mothballs,
this open cage,
this broken wood from Tule Lake.
I keep these like a rock
in my shoe
to remind me not to weep,
to mend my own body,
to wait not for the entry of men
or ghosts.
I claim
my place
in this line of
generations of women,
lean with work,
soft as tea,
open as the tunnels of the sea
driven as the heels of freedom's feet.
Taut fisted with reparations.

Mother, grandmother
speak in me.
I claim their strong fingers
of patience, their knees
bruised with humiliation,
their hurt, longing,
the sinews of their survival.
Generations of yellow women
gather in me
to crush the white wall
not with the wearing of sorrow
not with the mildew of waiting,
not with brooding or bitterness or regret,
not with wilted flowers or red lipstick.
We crush
the white wall
with a word, a glance,

a garden new with golden bamboo,
juniper with barbed wire at their root,
splinters from barracks.
We will come like autumn shedding sleep
a sky about to open with rage,
thunder on high rocks.
I crush
the white wall
with my name.

> *Pronounce it correctly*
> *I say*
> *Curl it on their tongue*
> *Feel each and many*
> *syllable of it,*
> *like grains of warm rice*
> *and that will be pleasing.*

Generations of women
spilling each syllable
with a loud, yellow noise.

1983

MS.

I got into a thing
with someone
because I called her
miss ann/hearst/rockerfeller/hughes
instead of ms.

I said
it was a waste of time
worrying about it.

Her lips pressed white
thinning words like pins
pricking me – a victim of sexism.

I wanted to
call her what
she deserved
but knowing it would please her
instead
I said,

> white lace & satin was never soiled by
>   sexism
> sheltered as you are by mansions
>   built on Indian land
>
> your diamonds shipped with slaves from Africa
> your underwear washed by Chinese launderies
> your house cleaned by my grandmother

so do not push me any further.

And when you quit
killing us
for democracy
and stop calling ME *gook*.

I will call you
whatever you like.

1977

LULLABYE

My mother merely shakes
her head
when we talk about the war,
the camps,
the bombs.

She won't discuss
the dying/her own
as she left her self
with the stored belongings.

She wrapped her shell
in kimono sleeves
and stamped it third class
delivery to Tule Lake

> *futokoro no ko*
> > *child at my breast*
> *oya no nai*
> > *parentless*

What does it mean to be citizen ?

> *It is privilege*
> *to pack only what you can carry*

> *It is dignity*
> *to be interned for your own good*

> *It is peace of mind*
> *constituted by inalienable right*

She x'd the box marked "other"

pledging allegiance
to those who would have turned
on the gas mercifully

> *Her song:*
> *shikata ga nai*
>> *it can't be helped*

She rode on the train
destined for omission
with an older cousin

who died next to her
gagging when her stomach burned out.

Who says you only die once ?

> My song:

> *Watashi ga kadomo wa matte eru*
> *I am a child waiting*
>> *waiting*

> *Watashi no hahaga umareta*
>> *for the birth of my mother.*

1976

AUGUST 6

Yesterday
a thousand cranes
were flying.
Hiroshima,
your children
still dying

        and they said

        it saved many lives

the great white heat
that shook flesh from bone
melted bone
to dust

        and they said
        it was merciful

yesterday
a thousand cranes
were flying.
Obachan
offered omame
to her radiant Buddha
incense smoking miniature
mushrooms
her lips moving
in prayer
for sister they found
tattooed to the ground
a fleshless shadow on Hiroshima soil

        and they said
        Nagasaki

Yesterday
a woman
bore a child
with fingers
growing from her neck
shoulder
empty

                    and they said
                    the arms race

Today
a thousand cranes
are flying
and in expensive waiting rooms
of Hiroshima, California
are blood counts
sucked by the white death

                    and they said
                    it might happen again

tonight
while
everyone sleeps
memoryless
the night wind
flutters like a thousand wings
how many ears will hear
the whisper
"Hiroshima"
from a child's
armless shoulder
puckered
like a kiss ?

1978

SING WITH YOUR BODY

for my daughter, Tianne Tsukiko

We love with great difficulty
spinning in one place
afraid to create
                    spaces
                            new rhythm

the beat of a child
dangled by her own inner ear
takes Aretha with her

                    upstairs, somewhere

go quickly, Tsukiko,

                    into your circled dance
go quickly

                    before your steps are
                    halted by who you are not

go quickly

                    to learn the mixed
                    sounds of your tongue,

go quickly

                    to who you are

                    before

your mother swallows
what she has lost.

1975

Late With Lunch

LATE WITH LUNCH

"Wife is late with the lunch . . .
kills herself . . ."

UPI dateline, Seoul, Korea
San Francisco Chronicle, May 12, 1987

She washes
in the wooden tub,
pouring water to purify her hands.
Incense burns slowly.
She has swept and wiped
the floor clean,
smoothing white sheets
pulled from her bed over
the polished wood.
She fingers the leather
beltstrap worn and bloodstained
hanging from his closet door.
He would use it when he was sober.
When he drank,
he desired to feel my flesh,
the soft crunch of my face bones
on his bare knuckles,
hear the thudding echo his fists made on my skull.
He would wash down the taste of blood
with the vodka he sloshed
in his mouth as he sucked
my broken lips.
The soberness of the strap allows
him the distance
to torture me,
as he pulls me to him, tethered
by the leather leash.

The strap allows him more control
without bruising his fists,
without spattering my blood.
He would, at the precise hour,
require her to serve him
tea, hot rice, thin slices of raw
red meat over green burning wasabi.
He would have her wear her kimono
with tight obi to demonstrate
her obedience
to his friends.   He boasted
that he has never had to wait
for his meal.
That day,
she went to the market
to buy fresh oranges and fish
for his lunch,
forgot to forward her clock for daylight
saving time.
One hour late,
she came home to an empty house,
the only message he left
was the beltstrap tied to the neck
of her teapot
spilling its dregs of leaves.
She washes her hands
once more, kneels on the white sheets
and carefully arranges
the platter of raw meat, a hot bin of rice,
tea, in the center of the floor
beneath the ceiling beam
where the strap is hooked.
The belt
snaps her neck
as she kicks away the chair.

Her twitching legs
spray her feces over steaming white rice
and shatters the teapot.

It is the precise hour
of his dinner meal.
He returns.

My husband,
may this length of strap
that hangs me,
the evidence of your cruelty,
be the distance
I hold you to me,
forever.

LYDIA

      sat up from her bed,
      vomited in the bucket
      and guzzled again
      from her bottle of fortified wine.
They brought me to her because I was drinking too much,
my friends who said she was
a woman of water, dwelling between worlds.
In her room,
a dresser with framed photographs,
a tapestry of buffalo,
sand paintings,
the rank odor of vomit.
      Her long, bone thin finger
      curled into her palm
      dragged across the sheets, telling me come close,
      her flesh closing around her eyes,
      her skin rusted red from throttled kidneys.
      Her hair is scant and patchy, and when she smiles
      her gums are flaming with loose teeth.
She points to the photograph of a young woman
who is smiling, cheeks smooth,
eyes black, shining
and her thick braided hair is held sleek by
a beaded orange head band.
I have never seen such a beautiful woman.
      Lydia vomits once more and laughs
      in the horizon of her sheets, the abyss of her bucket,
      "That is me," she gulps, her throat bobbing
      up and down like a boat.
         "THAT IS ME," she says, pointing to the photograph.
      And she says, pointing to herself,
         "THIS IS YOU."

'Lydia' reprinted from NO HIDING PLACE, by Rev. Cecil Williams
Harper Collins Publishers, New York, NY 10022,1992.

WRONG PLACE, WRONG TIME

In my window, a cobalt blue bowl
of bright tangerines.
She brought them to me for luck, on the New Year.
Gung hay fat choy . . .
She would have come sooner but her aunt's grandson
was shot in the spray of drive-by bullets,
as he brought home groceries . . . a good boy
who did not shoot guns.
No luck, she screamed, as she tore out her hair.
     Wrong place. Wrong time.
On the six o'clock news
I was struck by the limp body,
pulled by her sleeve, rolling cooperatively
onto a truck bed. Sixty-eight died
in the marketplace when war
as affectionate as shrapnel, mortar fire
split melons amidst scattered limbs
of children, women who were squeezing fruit
a moment before.
   Wrong place. Wrong time.
In my room that smells of tea and tangerines, roses
tinted like flesh, I want to forget
the time, the place
of dogs sniffing through torn bodies and melon seeds,
in a Sarajevo marketplace,
and a Detroit, Atlanta, Los Angeles, Bensenhurst, Oakland
sidewalk cluttered with oranges
and blood
and an unlucky
grandson's body.

1994

DOREEN

Doreen had a round face.
She tried to change it.
Everybody made fun
of her in school.

Her eyes so narrow
they asked if she could see,
called her moonface and
slits.

Doreen frost tipped her hair
ratted it five inches high,
painted her eyes round,
glittering blue shadow up to her brow.

Made her look sad
even when she smiled.

She cut gym all the time
because the white powder on her neck
and face would streak
when she sweat.

But Doreen had boobs
more than most of us Japanese girls
so she wore tight sweaters
and low cut dresses
even in winter.

She didn't hang
with us,
since she put so much time
into changing her face.

White boys
would snicker when she passed by
and word got around
that Doreen
went all the way,
smoked and drank beer.

She told us
she met a veteran
fresh back from Korea.

Fresh back
his leg
still puckered pink
from landmines.

She told us
it was a kick
to listen to his stories
about how they'd torture
the gooks
hang them from trees
by their feet
grenades
in their crotch
and watch
them sweat.

I asked her
why she didn't dig brothers.

And her eyes
would disappear
laughing
so loud
she couldn't hear herself.

One day,
Doreen riding fast
with her friend
went through the windshield
and tore off
her skin
from scalp to chin.

And we were sad.

Because
no one could remember
Doreen's face.

1987

. . . An Asian American college student was reported to have jumped to her death from her dormitory window. Her body was found two days later under a deep cover of snow. Her suicide note contained an apology to her parents for having received less than a perfect four point grade average . . .

SUICIDE NOTE

How many notes written . . .
ink smeared like birdprints in snow.

not good enough not pretty enough not smart enough
dear mother and father.
I apologize
for disappointing you.
I've worked very hard,
not good enough
harder, perhaps to please you.
If only I were a son, shoulders broad
as the sunset threading through pine,
I would see the light in my mother's
eyes, or the golden pride reflected
in my father's dream
of my wide, male hands worthy of work
and comfort.
I would swagger through life
muscled and bold and assured,
drawing praises to me
like currents in the bed of wind, virile
with confidence.
not good enough not strong enough not good enough

I apologize.
Tasks do not come easily.
Each failure, a glacier.

Each disapproval, a bootprint.
Each disappointment,
ice above my river.
So I have worked hard.
                    not good enough.
My sacrifice I will drop
bone by bone, perched
on the ledge of my womanhood,
fragile as wings.
                    not strong enough
It is snowing steadily
surely not good weather
for flying – this sparrow
sillied and dizzied by the wind
on the edge.
                    not smart enough.
I make this ledge my altar
to offer penance.
This air will not hold me,
the snow burdens my crippled wings,
my tears drop like bitter cloth
softly into the gutter below.
     not good enough not strong enough not smart enough

                    Choices thin as shaved
                    ice. Notes shredded
                    drift like snow

on my broken body,
covers me like whispers
of sorries
sorries.
Perhaps when they find me
they will bury
my bird bones beneath

a sturdy pine
and scatter my feathers like
unspoken song
over this white and cold and silent
breast of earth.

JADE JUNKIES

They called her Mamasan Kiru.
She could do anything with a knife.
Gut shrimp
with a single slice
dice
an onion before a tear
could slide.
Make cucumber history
each stroke quick
like a blink
thinner than your skin.
Her knuckles
were scarred from so many
nicks.
Some say she was cut deep
when her G.I. split
and left her
in the middle of America.
She couldn't go back home
in disgrace
so she carved out a place,
her one counter cafe
long before sushi
became fashionable
to jade junkies.
She'd dip her fingers
in ginger sauce
leave her scent
in raw bits of flesh
to make them crave
her flavor.
She'd slip fish
from scale to skin
before blood could think
to surface.

Yea, they'd stand in line
to see her magic
with a knife
scale,   skin
    slice
dice,
    chop.

And they'd always ask,
Do you orientals
do everything
so neatly?

IT ISN'T EASY

For Cecil

I want to give you
everything
yet nothing . . .
        my silence
a cup of tea,
chatter . . .
        the ants
invading our cannisters,
dishes piled like angry words,
dust gathering in corners
like unswept thought . . .
        It would be easier
this smallness of giving,
this reduction to detail
of maintenance:
the attention to
stockings that need mending,
the filling up of holes,
the knitting of emptiness.
        It would be easier
to be your victim.
Seduced by complacency
effortless acquiescence.
Let you pilot my passive
body into unknown ports . . .
abdicate to the whirling air
of your arms, and unresisting,
be tossed into the haunches of midnight.
        I want to give you
nothing,
yet everything:
the dreams I navigate
lapping on the shores of

Honshu to the Ivory Coast,
the hibiscus blooming
between my thighs,
          my poems
strung like bloody beads across my throat,
my disembowelment, my seppuku –
scarlet entrails
twisting from the open wound,
          my dark words
unbridled like horses
steaming nostrils, hoof, mane.

          It isn't easy
to bring to your hands
a storm of bloodred flowers
and brutal birthings,
          not easy
this passion for power, my unbeautiful hunger,
this selfish desire to be loud, bigger
than light, this longing
for movement, my own,
this discovery of unveiled women
rising up,
and tongueless ones
rising up . . .
          this rising up
through empty sockholes,
teacups, dishes, antfilled cannisters,
dust and acquiescence.

          It isn't easy
this love rising up
beside your great expanse.

Each lifting its own air,
yellow
dark
feathered flight,
filling the sky
with color and strange song.
A dazzle of independence.

It isn't easy.

1985

THE LOVERS

The man came
in from the field.
He said nothing
to the woman
and began to eat
that which she prepared for him.
They moved,
carefully
inevitably
as the silent keeping
of time.

For them,
it moved nowhere
but to etch lines
on the woman's face,
the man's hands.
"The plums are small"
is all he said.
The woman,
facing the man,
speechless,
poured the steaming tea
slowly to half cup.
        (The steam,
        ghosting her vision,
        her desire
        her unspoken words:)
        I will start with your
        hands,
        and slowly
        with the sickle
        slice the folds
        of each finger

so blood will
form patterns
like the scales of fish.
Then I will hold the slivers
of flesh
and peel them slowly
as we do the skin of ripe
plums
until your eyes
widen with the pain
until the bone
appears like hope.
You will wince
as I approach
your face
with my razor sharp
fish knife
and carve your cheekbones
leaving only the flesh
around your eyebrows
shaped like wings.
And your eyes,
that are indifferent like the dead
will come alive
with horror/seeing me
for the first time.

Listen, listen
I will whisper
to the rhythm of your blood
rippling like the river
that feeds your plums.

The man gazes up
at her,
    (she is straddling him
    with the blade between her teeth
    a love never seen before
    in his smile)
he does not smile.
    (and he will say:)

        I hear the singing of plums
        drinking the earth,
        sucking the sun.
        You have kept your breasts
        hidden from me
        in darkness.
        I could only feel
        the ripe smooth bursting
        as I entered
        the root place
        between your thighs.
        Silence has been my defense
        of your woman masterhood.

        The trees are my friends.
        What they ask of me,
        I can give.
        What I plant
        I get back.
        What I nourish
        I eat.
        Entering the house
        with you in your silent
        making
        your suffocating
        servitude,

I will pull with my strong neck
the plow blade,
you, like the shaft of wheat
slipping to the threshing
floor
scattered there like seed.
I will run the blade
first up the sides
of your thighs
until your blood
has grained the wood.

The woman, wordless,
pours his tea
silently.

The man,
eyes indifferent like the dead
says,
"The plums are small
this year."

1983

CRAZY ALICE

Aunt Alice, who has touched the sun . . .
victim of American concentration camps

She came to the
wedding
in a tattered coat
called us all by
the wrong names

Yukio/Mizume/Kyoko

No, crazy Alice
We died in the camps

                              remembering/remembering
                              Alice/back then

and the relatives
laughed behind
her back/crazy Alice

                              the bride is beautiful
                              who is she?

crazy Alice
it is your daughter

                              okashi ne
                              jinsei wa okashi

                              life's so strange
                              before the war
                              i had a name

twenty years ago
she would come to us
face blue
eyes like black walnuts

and down her nose
blood flowed like tears

battered by husbands
and lovers
for hoarding food
and love

where has love gone?

        the children
        will starve
        remember the war
        eating potato roots

and thinking of
invasions
and prison camps
she opened her legs
to the white boss man

        okashi ne
        jinsei wa okashi

        life's so strange
        before the war
        i had a name

crazy Alice
where do you wander ?
you walk on the sun
your eyes
keep the years
motionless
and your tears like rain
on a sleeping sea

        my child is hungry
        what will i do

crazy Alice
    crazy Alice

she is the bride
standing before you

                    my child is dead
                    my breasts dried
                    during the war
                    and she died
                    from hunger

rejoice
Crazy Alice/your child
has a new name

                    okashi ne, okashi
                    Jinsei wa okashi

                    life's so strange
                    before the war
                    i was my child
                    i had a name

1976

DROWNING IN THE YELLOW RIVER

Necking in back seats

of convertibles with white boys
while elvis
creams out your pain

                                screams out your song
                                "you ain't nothin' but a . . ."

who else am i?

The silk scarf obachan
gave you
you wear like ann margaret
in convertible winds

                                flapping to
                                "don't step on my . . ."

who else am i?

look at me –
buddaheads
chinamen who stand
on one side of the room
and don't mess with girls

who else am i?

necking is so hard
in the back seat
with white boys
had to pee so bad
crossing your legs

                    elvis panting
                    "don't be cruel"

she couldn't say
stop suckin' on my neck daddy-o
gotta go
to the obenjo

                    one once asked if jap toilets
                    had horizontal plumbing

who else am i?

crossing your legs
slid the silk scarf
into your crotch

                    elvis stops for a commercial
                    "wonder where the yellow went . . ."

obachan's silk scarf
sucked the yellow river
you came home
rumpled
hickied

(he'll call you again sometime)

you hung
your yellowed
pee-drowned scarf to dry

who else am i?

1978

Tongues Afire

WAR OF THE BODY

for Cecil

*"There is nothing too awful, too
shameful to tell at Glide. In truth,
there is NO HIDING PLACE . . ."*
Cecil Williams

I had hoped for a truce
not believing it possible,
this protracted war with my body,
so long waged, hating my breasts
that stung to the touch,
this flat body, frigid as a bivouac.
I had feared no marriage
could survive my demolition.

       From her childhood,
       the invasions of male artillery without warning
       at night when stars were hidden,
       excavated, scudmissiled her.
       Like a prisoner of war, she crept into
       sweet, unchallenging silence
       where she could escape,
       leave from the village of her body
       and watch it burn from a distance.
       She wished the mothers
       would rescue the children at least,
       clutch them to their backs,
       and carry them to safety.
       But he quickly scattered them like a fallen nest,
       broken eggshells, twigs, feathers,
       crushed by his heavy bootheel.
       He grinds the child into the soft wood
       of her cage, until her back
       is a wall of slivers.

He captures chickens, rubs his fingers into them,
molests the kittens, dogs in heat, as they hiss, howl,
often die. He laughs, knowing that the child sees.

I tell you these memories,
yielding my silence like a weapon,
as we vault through minefields of marriage,
my rage meaner than mortar,
thoughtless as prison food.
My body, like a burn victim
is cauterized shut.
I tell you in the warm sunlight of morning,
your eyes swarming like bees.
You say the dead can spring from our throats.
You have laid your face into burnt soil,
seen leaves rotting like flesh,
but from the bones sprout lavender,
henna, elm.
You whisper Isaiah to me, "*Rain does not return*
to heaven until it waters earth."*

     Everything is useful.
     Come, you say,
bring your slivered wall,
your burned village,
your amputated sex, the prisons of silence,
your torn bird
to my sanctuary.
     No secret is too shameful.
Place your soiled breasts
into the nest of my hands.
Truth is not punished here
in this demilitarized zone
where you are not a segregated woman
but an integrity of light.

---

*Quote from Bible, Isaiah 55:10.

My body
in the forest of your arms,
becomes unseparated,
as I pull your mouth
to my throat
so that I may have two tongues.
I breathe with your breathing.
My flesh opens, unstitched.
Hair flows the length of sheets,
and the oils of our skin
blend like two streams joining.

This river is clean.
On the shore at this moment
the child is clutched on my back,
being carried to safety.

June 6, 1993
Wales

LETTER TO MY DAUGHTER

You have left home.
Not when expected nor desired,
but most probably at the right time.
I finger the hem of the short skirt
you left behind, sigh at the empty phone socket,
and hear the echoes of rock music
crashing off your empty walls.
I wonder at the chasm between us and weep
for my loss.
Ah, that I could mend and bridge
those silences you built
like garrisons to protect the fragile
blooming of your self.
So I ask, what would I give to you, my daughter?

My jade ring? My pearl necklace?
The blue kimono handed down by my mother?
China cups brought from Japan, survivors of canefields
and concentration camps,
grandmother's mottled and dented pot
used to nourish generations?
Daughter, I want you to know
the compassion of an old pot.
She would feed everyone: children,
dogs, chickens, sheep –
no matter what – drought, poverty, bill collectors.
We didn't know how she did it,
out of almost nothing –
gizzards, chicken feet, fishheads, greens,
from grandmother's pot came feasts.
It was in her daily certainty, to sustain us,
repeated like ritual, that we understood the reliance
of one creature upon the other – each a part unto the whole,
deserving the fundamental act of care.
They found her in the barn

crumpled beneath a sack of mash.
"Past feeding time," she groaned.
Despite the hump
on her crippled back,
the joints twisted with arthritis and age,
she kept her hands
open like spoons.
What else, daughter?
Memory.   that instills passion and
connectedness.

My mother, a lovely ribbon in a field of soil,
her hands delicate like camellias,
thought she would escape the drudgery of the farm,
and dreamed her dreams to become a singer.
In America, land of opportunity.
Except for "all persons of Japanese Ancestry"
locked behind barbed wire. She didn't
sing anymore. It was like somewhere in her
core, someone spit – Filthy Jap –
made her recoil, and that part of her died,
and though the hurt rippled on her tongue
she swallowed all of it
choking it back,
holding it down,
never to release those bitter notes.
Racism and war and abandonments
made her fearful of loss.
She saves everything now. Stamps, aluminum foil,
coupons, string. Collecting loose strands,
she rolls patiently into a ball, tying end to end.
I unravel the tangled threads
of my life, inextricably tied to hers.
For so long I blamed her for my knots
of insecurity, worthlessness. How easy to blame her,
rather than look at myself.
It was not my mother who tied the cord of dependence
around my neck. She did not delude me into thinking

I am nothing without a man.
Her history is a lesson
for my freedom.   And yours, my daughter.
What do I want for you?
To know the necessity of struggle.
The absence of struggle is death . . . do not be lulled
into passivity and indifference,
self indulgence and isolation.
We live in a society that seduces
us into complacency, mindless consumerism.
The anaesthetics of drugs. Instant gratification.
Easy answers, materialism.
A society that threatens we should not
make disturbances.
Insidious racism that tells us
we are conditionally acceptable only if we fit
into their mold of the model minority.
The one dimensional caricature
houseboy/oriental chick without history
or ability or thought.
Do not accept the exoticized/china doll/
geisha girl/can't tell you apart/
good in math/you speak English so well/
death of a rebel.
Remember, daughter, that not one generation ago
we were the expendable ones,
denied justice,
incarcerated for the "crime" of ancestry,
the barbed wire of those camps is still
wrapped around my heart.
The scars from wounds must become memory.
Listen to the stories. We are the heroes
and sheroes in the pages we write, the songs
we compose, the testimonies we claim.
They will save our lives, make you proud.
They will extend to you
the hands of justice

that must expand from El Salvador to Soweto,
from Tiananmen Square to Azerbaijan,
from a bloody Stockton schoolyard to the bloody streets
of Howard Beach, from the tenements of refugees
to the homeless shelters of the Tenderloin
to the reservations of Pine Ridge.

      What do I want for you, my daughter?
      The courage to join these hands.
      For your ends of string are inextricably tied
      one to the other, to the suffering and the hungry,
      the unknown, and the victorious ones.
      One to the other, mother, grandmother, you.
      Their struggle has insured our survival.
      Their love has birthed your possibilities.
      What do I want for you, daughter?
To continue to tie
generation to generation these threads of memory,
to bind each other in justice,
to mend with love,
and always
with your own voice
to sing your song.

HAIKU

For David Charlsen

Mirror, ink, paper.
What you give to me —
letters to calligraph voice,
courage to push, breathe.

My face looks less
like your face
the older I get,
mine threatened with
shadowed lines.
          Perhaps it is because
          you keep gathering children
          to your lap,
          feed them undivided
          affection, brightly colored
          eggs, stories,
          laughter,
          books of art, an opening
          in the world,
that light expands
around you.
          You know about the child
          who counted stars,
          a ritual to stave
          cruelty,
          so many children of the dark,
          praying for light.
I bring my face
of graying words
to you,
and some milk
          for you've grown big
          against the sky.

Burst with birthings.
A child comes rolling out
amidst
stars
gathering.

WHAT MATTERS

The things that matter
you ask, where is love?
The poem
soft as linen
dried by the sun?
words of comfort
like puffed pillows
yellow flowers
with velvet petals?
Where is serenity,
cherry blossoms arranged,
the quaint ceremony of tea?
Images metaphysically deep
spoken in Japanese,
preferably seventeen syllables of

       persimmons or new
       plums or snow covered bridges
       or red flow of leaves?

What matters
the trickling clarity of
water
each day, not fearing thirst.
    I love you
when persimmons sweat
shining in a sand gray bowl,
    Mama
hiding pennies
under floor boards
with flour, saltine crackers,
balls of used aluminum foil,
string, coupons and water jars
secreted for that day.
That day

when all would be taken
and packing
must be quick again.
      I love you
when snow covers the bridge
curved over ice white water,
      Grandfather
killing my cat
who ripped open his hens,
sucking their eggs.
His eyes, half closed
behind steel rims,
cigarette holder
clenched in his teeth,
as he fondled the rock.
Before I could cry
or plead,
my cat, writhing
with skull crushed.
He captured a rabbit,
gave it to me
and warned
we would eat in winter
as soon as I began to love her.

      I love you
when plums burst like new moons,
crescents on their black boughs,
      my husband
whose dark hands
embrace the wilted shoulders
of the wretched,
winos with wracked eyes,
and welfare mothers cleaning cockroaches
from the lips of their children.
His words
like spoons, nourishing.

I love you
when leaves flow in crimson,
orange, yellow, sepia waves,
    my daughter
who weeps for each dead
seal, murdered tiger,
cat's corpse, endangered species
of condor and chinese panda,
crusading against gamesmen
and trophy hunters.
    What matters,
Breath
for the shipwrecked, drowning.
    What matters
amidst the dread of nuclear winter,
Chernobyl's catastrophe, Three Mile Island,
Nevada's test veterans, terrorism,
the massacred in Port Elizabeth, the
wounded of Central America, genocide of drugs,
AIDS, toxic waste, Atlanta's missing
and mutilated*, hunger, mistaken identities,
murder in the streets.
    A love poem?

    Clear water passing   (5)
    our mouths unafraid to breathe,   (7)
    and to speak freely   (5)

1980

---

*In 1979 in Atlanta, Georgia, police began investigating a rash of disappearances. By May 1981, twenty-eight young African Americans, mostly children, had been found murdered. A twenty-ninth victim is still missing. Wayne Williams was convicted of two of the killings, and was implicated in twenty-two others. He will be eligible for parole in 1996.

FOR GRANDMOTHER

Today, when April rain
spills into the sad eyes
of my room,
grandmother returns,
her porcelain dish
on my table abiding,
saved from among her belongings.
>How many journeys?
>Hiroshima
>Hawaii's canefields
>California's scratchland
>Amache Gate*
She comes
when the silences are white glass,
a single crane painted resolute
to find her mate,
holding forever the white wind in her wing.
>Earth
>Pine
>Sky
Grandmother,
immutable porcelain dish,
translucent at its rim, like the world's edge
where birds flying,
flying they sing —

Your eternal journey is chiseled
in our bones.

---

*Amache Gate One of ten American concentration camps in which over 110,000 persons of
Japanese ancestry, mostly American citizens, were incarcerated during World War II.

HER FACE

For Maya Angelou

> "Love affords wonder
> because it gives us the courage / liberty
> to go inside and see who we are really . . ."
> *Maya Angelou*

The woman rolls away
stones from our tombs.
The silence of the grave
is broken.
Some of us
have been told to keep quiet,
hold our tongues,
convinced we have no mouths,
incapable of shaping words
because none would be believed.
It was forbidden to reveal family
secrets, not polite to disrupt the conspiracy,
uncomfortable. Dangerous.
People would die.
Our mothers abandoned. It would be our
fault. We buried
our voices
deeper into the puckers of self-blame.
But the woman at the open tomb
with throat full of grace
tells us truth.
She writes stories within her skin,
carries their songs in her long body,
her rhythms leap into our soul's
lining.
We cannot keep still.
Her face is familiar,
radiates all colors of the rainbow.

Her words breaking like light,
a bird's full wing,
allure a sunrise,
wind on free blue water.

The tombs of silence
are emptied. She informs us
that death cannot detain us,
she loves even me and she and he
and we. Her face
is familiar
       the face of a woman who laughs
       the one who calls each of us by name.
       She who brings fruit to the asylum, singing to misfits.
       The woman who takes nothing from her journey,
       she who marches for peace, all freedoms,
                     liberating the children.
       She who does not tolerate brutality.
       The one who writes poetry for all of a nation.
Language is released
that all understand.
       "Love affords wonder . . ." Maya Angelou says.
We are arranging our faces.
Our mouths bloom with orchids and simple words,
elegant words.

Hope surrounds us.

SOUL FOOD

For Cecil

We prepare
the meal together.
I complain,
hurt, reduced to fury
again by their
subtle insults
insinuations
because I am married to you.
Impossible autonomy, no mind
of my own.

You like your fish
crisp, coated with cornmeal,
fried deep,
sliced mangos to sweeten
the tang of lemons.
My fish is raw,
on shredded lettuce,
lemon slices thin as skin,
wasabe burning like green fire.
You bake the cornbread flat
and dip it in
the thick soup
I've brewed from
turkey carcass, rice gruel,
sesame oil and chervil.
We laugh over watermelon
and bubbling cobbler.

You say,
there are few men
who can stand
to have a woman equal,
upright.

This meal,
unsurpassed.

1987

BREAKING TRADITION

For my daughter

My daughter denies she is like me,
her secretive eyes avoid mine.
    She reveals the hatreds of womanhood
    already veiled behind music and smoke and telephones.
I want to tell her about the empty room
    of myself.
    This room we lock ourselves in
    where whispers live like fungus,
    giggles about small breasts and cellulite,
    where we confine ourselves to jealousies,
    bedridden by menstruation.
    This waiting room where we feel our hands
    are useless, dead speechless clamps
    that need hospitals and forceps and kitchens
    and plugs and ironing boards to make them useful.
I deny I am like my mother. I remember why:
    She kept her room neat with silence,
    defiance smothered in requirements to be otonashii*,
    passion and loudness wrapped in an obi,
    her steps confined to ceremony,
    the weight of her sacrifice she carried like
    a foetus. Guilt passed on in our bones.
I want to break tradition – unlock this room
    where women dress in the dark.
    Discover the lies my mother told me.
    The lies that we are small and powerless
    that our possibilities must be compressed
    to the size of pearls, displayed only as
    passive chokers, charms around our neck.

---

*Japanese word for "nice, well behaved."

Break Tradition.
> I want to tell my daughter of this room
> of myself
> filled with tears of shakuhachi,
>> the light in my hands,
>> poems about madness,
>> the music of yellow guitars,
>> sounds shaken from barbed wire and
>> goodbyes and miracles of survival.

> My daughter denies she is like me
>> her secretive eyes are walls of smoke
>> and music and telephones.
>> her pouting ruby lips, her skirts
>> swaying to salsa, Madonna and the Stones.
>> her thighs displayed in carnavals of color.
>> I do not know the contents of her room.
> She mirrors my aging.

> She is breaking tradition.

1985

TOMATOES

"We have to read The Red Badge of Courage*"*
"We all had to read it."
"But all heroes are not men."
Dialogue with my daughter

Hanako loved her garden. She and her young daughter lived with her parents on a farm planted in the stretch of fields near Gilroy. Her husband died during the war. He was a hero. Received medals and letters of commendation for valor in battle, for defending his country, for saving fellow soldiers in his regiment.

Hanako had delivered to her an American flag and his medal after she and her parents got out of the concentration camp located in the middle of the desert.

When they returned to her parent's farm, the house had to be repaired and rebuilt and the land was dried, cracked like weathered skin.

Hanako would look out over the wide flat expanse of the valley. In the dry season it reminded her of the camp desert where the heat would shimmer up and if you looked long enough you thought you could see someone approaching. She'd do that a lot, dreaming her husband would be running toward her. She'd shade her eyes and watch as the sun pulsated, conjuring up the man with the strong warm hands that would go up her neck and through her hair and pull her face close to him. The heat from the ground would travel through her body and she would weep from the barrenness of knowing he would never be coming back.

Lisa looked like him, his squarish jaw, his deep black eyes, the smile lines in her cheek.

Mommy, I want red flowers.

Hanako set about to soften her earth, make her garden. She wielded her hoe like a sword, breaking hard crusts of dirt. Lisa would bring out the hose and buckets to help moisten the ground, playing in the water, muddy pools created by Hanako's shovel. She planted bright geraniums that grew sturdily in dry climate next to her tomato vines.

The Haufmanns who lived four acres away came over the day they returned to the farm, talked about the hard times they had during the war and difficulties in keeping up their own land. They just couldn't

afford to water anyone else's crops even with the extra money and the furniture, china, tractor, seedlings, livestock they were given by Hanako's parents before their hasty departure to the camps. Mr. Haufmann kicked the dirt as he commented that Hanako didn't look any the worse for wear. He eyed her breasts under her white cotton blouse, and admired how Lisa had grown into a fine young girl with slender hips like her mommy and so sorry
to hear about the husband.
    Hanako answered politely
> the war is over and done.
> We've come back to start our life again
> like planting new seeds and hoping they'll
> grow stronger.

    Mr. Haufmann would frequently visit if he'd see Hanako and Lisa in their resurrected garden, weeding, pulling the dandelion from her tender tomato vines, her sweet peas with their thin delicate stalks climbing the stakes she had hammered into the ground in neat rows, the robust thick stubs of kale, and Lisa's geraniums brightly red in the heat.
> Kinda delicate, aren't you, doing
> all this work? Skin's going to shrivel
> in this mean sun. Work's too heavy for little girls.
    Hanako would stand up straight and speak politely, softly,
> there are many things we must learn
> to do without
> and find the strength
> to do ourselves.
    Lisa, tending her flowers, ran up to Mr. Haufmann who lifted her high in the air, her skirt flying above her panties. Mr. Haufmann laughing, flinging her up again and again, until Hanako would tell Lisa to finish her watering chores, her eyes turning black and silent as she whacked at the heads of dandelion weeds with her hoe.
    The heat rose early that day, its fingers clutching the rows of dirt. Hanako from the kitchen window did not see Lisa in the garden, watering as she usually did. She went immediately outside, looking, instinctively picked up her hoe and walked through the shimmering heat.

Hanako started toward the Haufmann farm when she saw Lisa
running toward her with a paper bag.

> Mommy. Mommy. Mr. Haufmann
> gave me pears and figs. They're ripe
> and sweet. He let me climb and pick
> them myself. He's so strong, let me
> stand on his shoulders so I could reach
> the top branches.

Hanako's knuckles turned white on the handle of the hoe, told Lisa
she was not to play at the Haufmanns' again, returned to her garden and
sprayed for insects.

Mr. Haufmann appeared in the waves of heat that afternoon, wiping
off his face with the back of his hand. Hanako's sweat ran down her
back, popped above her mouth. Haufmann redfaced, smiling

> Tomatoes looking good and juicy.
> Got a lotta nice young buds gonna pop soon, too.
> Heat's good for them I guess.

Hanako with her hoe turned the soil gently,

> How's your wife? Haven't seen her for awhile.

Wetting his lips

> O, that old mare's too tired to
> walk even this distance. Just sits at the
> radio and knits. Damn knitting gets on
> my nerves.

Hanako's hoe, turning, turning

> And your sons. Are they doing well?

Haufmann's hard laugh

> Too good for farming. Both in college,
> and don't hardly write or call. Busy
> chasing women and getting into trouble.
> Ha. Rascals they are. Men will be men.

Hanako's hoe fiercely cutting near the tomato vines

> You are fortunate to have healthy children.

Hanako's hoe high in the air, whacked like a sword through a ripe
tomato, juices springing up, smearing the soil

> There's nothing we won't do
> to insure their happiness, is there?

her voice low and glinting now like her blade as she whacked off the
head of another tomato smearing the handle red. Haufmann's eyes,
fading lights of blue, blinked as he stepped backward. Hanako's voice
now like the edge of sharp knives almost whispering

>We see so much of ourselves
>
>mirrored in our children
>
>except more . . .

Whack. Hanako's hoe now fiercely slicing, thudding, crushing the
ripened crop of tomatoes as the blade smeared red, the handle now
slippery with juices and pink seeds

>I have no bitterness Mr. Haufmann
>
>not about the war, nor the losses.

She thought of her husband's final moments.
Did he suffer long. What were his thoughts . . .

>the humiliation of those camps.

Did he remember her and their chubby Lisa waving from the wire
fence as he left them for the war?

>the work or this heat
>
>or the loneliness.
>
>Only the regret
>
>that my husband

The memory of smile lines in his cheek,
his warm hands stroking Lisa's hair,
quieting her in his rocking arms.

>cannot see the growing,
>
>budding living hope

Lisa came running to her mother's side, speechless at the devastation,
the red mass of crushed tomatoes, her eyes wide and instantly older,
seeing Haufmann wilting
shriveled in sweat and the wrinkles
of his wet shirt.
He, wordless, slumped
to escape
into the waves of heat.

>Mother. I'm so glad
>
>you saved my geraniums.

1983

SHADOW IN STONE

Journey to Hiroshima, Japan
International Peace Conference, 1984

We wander in the stifling heat
of August.
Hiroshima,
your museum, peace park,
paper cranes rustling whispers
of hei-wa *peace*
Burning incense
throbbing with white chrysanthemums,
plum blossoms, mounds
of soundless bones.
Hiroshima
how you rise up
in relentless waves of heat.
I come to you late,
when the weather bludgeons, blisters.
      I put my mouth
on your burning sky
on the lips of your murmuring river.
Motoyasu, river of the dead.

      The river speaks:
          I received the bodies
          leaping into my wet arms
          their flesh in flame, and the flies
          that followed
          maggots in the bloated sightless waste,
          skin rotting like wet leaves.
          My rhythm stifled, my movement stilled.

Motoyasu cries with rituals,
bearing a thousand flickering candles
in floating lanterns of yellow, red, blue

to remember the suffering.
I light a lantern for grandmother's sister
whom they never found amidst the ashes
of your cremation.
She floats beside the other souls
as we gather, filling water
in the cups of our hands,
pouring it back into the thirsty mouths
of ghosts, stretching parched throats.

The heat presses like many hands.
I seek solace in the stone
with human shadow burned into its face.
      I want to put my mouth to it
to the shoulders of that body,
my tongue to wet its dusty heart.

      I ask the stone to speak:
           When I looked up,
           I did not see the sun
           a kind friend who has gently pulled
           my rice plants skyward.
           I worried in that moment
           if my child would find shade
           in this unbearable heat
           that melts my eyes.
           No, I did not see the sun.
           I saw what today
           mankind has created
           and I layed my body
           into this cool stone,
           my merciful resting place.

Museum of ruins.
The heat wrings our bodies
with its many fingers.
Photographs remind us of a holocaust

and imagination stumbles, beaten, aghast.
I want to put my mouth
against these ruins, the distorted teacup,
crippled iron,
melted coins,
a disfigured bowl.

I ask the bowl to speak:
The old man
held his daughter,
rocking her in his lap,
day after day after
that terrible day,
she weak from radiation
could not lift this bowl.
Her face once bright like our sunset
now white as ash,
could not part her lips
as he tried to spoon okayu from this bowl
droplet by droplet
into the crack of her mouth,
the watered rice with umeboshi
which he would chew to feed her.
He did not know
when she stopped breathing
as he put his mouth to hers
gently to pass food.
He rocked her still body
watching the red sunset
burning its fiery farewell.

Hiroshima, rising up.
I come here late
when the weather sucks at us.
I want to put my mouth
to the air, its many fingers of heat,
lick the twisted lips

of a disfigured bowl,
the burned and dusty heart of shadow in stone,
put my mouth to the tongues
of a river,
its rhythms, its living water
weeping on the sides of lanterns,
each floating flame, a flickering
voice murmuring
over and over
as I put my mouth
to echo
over and over

  never again.

LOVE CANAL

And you will forget
even this
         the earth
         gray, its sickness
         bubbling
         through the cracked lips
         of packed dirt.
         Maria
         lays in her bed
         lined with mourners,
         suitors, priests, sons.
         In love,
         her eyes dropping
         sorrow,
         her pale gray hands
         thinned to the bone
         fingering the beads,
         hope emaciated like starved
         women.
         Maria,
         mother, lover.
         opening for them
         like a moist cave
         promising tomorrow,
         forever.

And you will forget
even this.
         They wound
         the heart,
         burn, pierce,
         bludgeon the breast
         of Love Canal.
         Her lips, lungs swell,
         heave, spit

Maria dreams
between her pain,
her skin burning,
cells screaming
armpits glowing
with bright embers
of radiation treatments.
He brought sunshine
like marigolds
into her lap
made her heart pump full
with rhythms of a young colt.
And in the streams
surrounding Love Canal,
they would dip, sip,
deep into each other's skin.
Her body
a canal for love
glistens with pain
sores like water
running to the edges of
her flesh.

And you will forget
even this

       Hooker Chemical Company
       pours the poison
       dumps its waste
       into vessels of earth
       at Love Canal.
       Mothers sip
       from its wells,
       children sleep
       in the fragrant air
       of buried waste,

                    fathers infertile
                    hum lullabys to unborn.
                    Maria awakens
                    from her toxic pillow
                    wet from the canal
                    of her polluted body,
                    flesh aflame,
                    bubbling pain,
                    like the angry earth
                    spewing sickness.

The priests and suitors
pray   fear no evil
              fear no evil
              fear evil
              evil . . .
over her body
once Love's Canal.

1983

TONGUES AFIRE

Upon hearing Dr. Maya Angelou
who moves us to remember

    You,

Your face like yellow roses,
you, honey colored,
nappy haired, curly, straight haired,
cropped, shaved, crimped, braided,
you remember the way women
walked in Dakar with baskets
on their heads, graceful
like palm trees swaying over
golden beaches.
      You, earth red colored faces, comforting
as shade,
you, brown and electric,
boneblack as the sands of Kona,
living on the cheeks of craters,
you remember the heat of creation.
      You, brilliant in red veils
from Bengal
even with lips blue from poison
indigo fields, plantations of death,
you remember rebellion, burning the slave holds.
      You with long black thighs,
marching the roads of Selma,
opening entrance to buses and schoolrooms,
facing racism's gnashing teeth,
you remember to laugh.
      You with faces of white gardenias,
remember the maimed but independent women
whose hands freed from knitting needles
and coathangers,
kindle the pathways of choice.

Our words like open wings
soar in spite of the pall of poverty,
the despair of shelters where light bulbs
are missing, dim rooms of broken mirrors,
I look at you and see my possibilities
in your beautiful faces.

We hold ourselves like candles.
Whispers of light gather.
Suddenly, we are blazing
with tongues afire.

Janice Mirikitani studied at the University of California at Los Angeles, the University of California at Berkeley, and at San Francisco State University. She is currently the Executive Director of Programs and President of Glide Church, a major multi-service/multi-cultural urban centre and church in San Francisco, where she lives with her husband, Rev. Cecil Williams and her daughter Tianne.